D1027325

CHAPTER 1

The Market

Autumn in Knox County, Illinois can be mesmerizingly beautiful as the foliage turns to hues of deep red, bright orange and golden yellow. The City of Galesburg, nestled in the center of the bucolic county, has long been recognized as a "tree city," with the city fathers having organized a tree department, adopted a tree ordinance and community forestry program, and made an annual Arbor Day proclamation. From the bell tower of the Central Congregational Church on the square in downtown Galesburg, you can observe the tremendous canopy of trees protecting the city's old neighborhoods for as far as the eye can see. That canopy covers a lot more than initially meets the eye.

A stone's throw from the Church, and under the departing shade of a pair of ancient oak trees partly responsible for that beautiful canopy, sits a small unassuming convenience store serving the residents of downtown Galesburg as well as those passing through town on Main Street, otherwise known as State Route 150. A veritable landmark in the small town, the market's storefront is showing its age and looks as though it may have been one of the first structures in the town, incorporated in 1857. The paint is peeling from the wooden trim, and the brick exterior could stand to be tuckpointed. The once green patina on the building's copper downspouts and gutters is turning black, and a tangle of ivy has overtaken those downspouts and clings mightily to the red brick exterior. But it proudly boasts an "open" sign in its front plate glass window, right below the large "SCHRODINGER'S MARKET" hand painted in giant glossy black lettering. As the leaves fall and dance in the slight wind swirling around the store entrance, the diminutive brick building emanates a glow from within, cascading its light over the gathering blanket of Fall leaves on the sidewalk and parking spaces in front of the market.

Two boys approached, precariously abandoning their bicycles near the entrance, and burst through the front door in search of candy bars and energy drinks. The gruff clerk, an elderly Korean man, gently scolded the boys for their parking job, but greeted them at the same time with a heartfelt "What can we do for you, gentlemen?" As the boys scoured the candy counter and hit the coolers for drinks, the clerk turned to continue his work of stocking cigarettes behind the counter while keeping a watchful eye on the youthful shoppers.

"Will that be all?" inquired the clerk as the boys approached the counter.

"This ought to do us." replied the older boy as he reached into his sweatshirt pocket for a small wad of bills.

Handing him his change, the clerk offered: "You boys should watch how much of that stuff you drink, you know." But, without response, the two boys were out of the store and back onto their bikes in a flash, their drinks and candy bars protruding from their pockets.

At 6 p.m., on this brisk November evening the light outside had substantially faded. The sun had set, and the streetlights struggled to supplement the dim moonlight visible from behind a thick layer of clouds. This left the bright lights of the market illuminating the clerk as he sat and read behind the counter, taking advantage of a brief lull in customer activity. The aroma of coffee and maple donuts permeated the tiny store which is old but tidy and stocked from floor to ceiling with essential merchandise. The tile floor gleamed in the ample florescent light. The yellow mop bucket in the corner stood witness to the efforts the owner still made to keep his establishment immaculate as his mentor had taught him decades ago.

The evening before Thanksgiving is always a bit busy at Schrodinger's Market, as people drop by to gather last minute items, not the least of which is booze. The owner had made sure to stock the cooler with, among other things, a large supply of forty-ounce cans of Schlitz Malt Liquor – becoming a neighborhood staple. One of the drinkiest nights of the year, Wednesday night before Thanksgiving, usually sees a good deal of revelry in downtown Galesburg as the several bars swell with patrons, including students back from college and members of the armed services home on leave for the holiday, all reuniting and catching up with friends and family.

In its one and a half centuries of existence, the market had been through several owners and facades, but each owner had seen fit to maintain the same name – that given to it by its founding owner, Thomas Schrodinger, a German-born immigrant. Schrodinger had moved to rural Knox County, Illinois from upstate New York in the mid nineteenth century to be part of the new utopian, abolitionist community of Galesburg.

Located at the center of the original city, the square is now a circle at the junction of Main and Broad Streets. The square is anchored by the Central Congregational Church, several aging bank buildings, a condemned hotel and other sundry retail store fronts. In the center of the square stands a bronze statue of the writer, poet and native son, Carl Sandburg, for whom the local community college is proudly named. Not far from the square to the south stands Old Main of Knox College the only structure still standing at which one of the famous Lincoln-Douglas debates was held on October 7, 1858. It was at Knox College that Abraham Lincoln famously stated that Stephen Douglas "is blowing out the moral lights around us, when he contends that whoever wants slaves has a right to hold them; that he is penetrating, so far as lies in his power, the human soul, and eradicating the light of reason and the love of liberty, when he is in every possible way preparing the public mind, by his vast influence, for making the institution of slavery perpetual and national."

But Galesburg has fallen on hard times with its manufacturing base decimated by the well intentioned North American Free Trade Agreement. The "giant whooshing sound" promised by Ross Perot was heard very loudly in this small mid-western factory town. And the city center shows it, as does the caliber of clientele who now frequent Schrodinger's Market. Galesburg is now primarily a town of old people and poor people – those who did not or could not escape the aftermath of globalization's negative impact on the area. The city's population, and that of the county, has been declining significantly for forty years. In his 2010 State of the Union Address, President Barack Obama offered Galesburg as an example given to the nation concerning those communities that had been left behind over the last few decades. Not a progressive municipality in recent years, Galesburg had taken no meaningful steps toward economic development to help balance or diversify its industrial and agricultural economy to weather the storm. A number of wise proposals for investment in the infrastructure of the community aimed at attracting businesses were dashed by the voters and City Councils over the years.

Instead, the City lobbied Springfield for a prison to be located there, and that wish was granted. Be careful what you wish for. A medium-security facility built in Galesburg soon became overcrowded with maximum security inmates primarily from the Chicago area. When the families of the inmates discovered that the cost of living in Galesburg was a mere fraction of that in Chicago, they moved to Galesburg where their assistance checks were just as generous, but they could now live much closer to their inmate son, brother or husband. Over time, the economic benefits of added employment provided by Henry C. Hill Correctional Facility turned into increased crime rates, gang activity and dysfunctional schools. This bad bargain did nothing to salve the wounds left by the departure of Maytag and Butler Manufacturing which relocated to greener pastures with lower labor rates and environmental regulations. But rather, it further strained local resources and made Galesburg a less livable town.

Nevertheless, Schrodinger's Market serves a real need in the community, providing patrons with coffee, cigarettes, condoms, snacks, rolling papers, grocery items, newspapers and lottery tickets. And it is also a sort of community center where people run into each other, stop to talk, and post pictures of missing dogs and help-wanted notes on the bulletin board.

Current owner, Glen Kim, had toiled in the market for fifty years. Glen was small in stature at approximately five feet six inches tall. He had a solid build and a strength that came from actively cleaning, stocking and working in his store. The physicality of the occupation was surprising. Lifting and moving large boxes of goods and mopping floors all day everyday was taxing, and Glen's body showed it. With dark hair and eyes, Glen was a handsome man. An only child, Glen was a naturalized American citizen having immigrated to the U.S. from South Korea in late 1965 at age 13. His parents had been casualties of the Korean War in the early 1950s. Glen had been sponsored by the Lutheran Ministries and raised by foster parents in Galesburg. He didn't talk about that experience very much. Glen worked as a clerk for the third owner of the market, Vernon Colton, a successful Galesburg entrepreneur who had hired the enterprising young Glen to help around the store with cleaning and stocking.

Eventually, Glen was able to purchase a half interest in the store from Mr. Colton, and upon Mr. Colton's death, he bequeathed the other half interest to Glen. Glen and his wife, Lin, with the assistance of their two daughters, Park and Yun, and his loyal employees, have operated the store ever since and through the turbulent times affecting the small city. Business was good enough that Glen and Lin were able to send their daughters to Knox College on scholarships and financial aid available to local students showing need and aptitude. The girls then moved to Chicago where they both married and experienced the type of success that metropolis can provide to hard working, ambitious young women. Glen remained enormously proud of his daughters and displayed an array of their graduation and wedding photos in full and prominent view behind the counter in his store.

But that night, Wednesday, November 24, there was something unusual in the air, an electricity that attends evenings preceding big holidays. The type of sense that anything could happen. The damp, cool Autumn air seemed to conduct that electricity throughout the town and those businesses that were still open. Everyone was wrapping up in the hopes of getting home early to begin the traditional Thanksgiving festivities. The bars a block over on Cherry Street were already teeming with merrymakers ringing in the celebration of family and the giving of thanks. But the atmosphere in Schrodinger's Market was calm and quiet with only the faint crackle of a police scanner in the background. A customer entered the store.

CHAPTER 2

The Event

"Johna McClay!" exclaimed Glen Kim, as the tall, athletic figure of a female Marine Corps Second Lieutenant pushed through the front door with a slightly embarrassed smile on her face. Lieutenant McClay was a young African American phenom whose athletic career Glen had followed in the local newspaper as she set record after record at both Galesburg High School and Knox College. She was a sprinter and hurdler of note in high school as well as an Academic All-American at college, where she participated in the ROTC program allowing her to join the U.S. Marine Corps as an officer following graduation. She was a standout to say the least. A real specimen. She was twenty-six years old.

"I haven't seen you for years, Johna. How've you been?" inquired Glen.

Johna had been a regular at Schrodinger's Market growing up and all through college, stopping by almost daily for odds and ends and her staple, YaHoo.

"Oh, Mr. Kim, I've missed you. I've been stationed in Afghanistan with the Second Battalion,

First Marine Regiment, First Marine Division until the withdrawal." replied Johna.

"I've missed reading about you in the local paper, Johna. And I've missed you coming in for your YaHoo!" stated Glen.

"I'm good ... just back on leave for the holiday, Mr. Kim." said Johna, as she approached the counter with a can of cherry pie filling. "Things haven't changed a whole lot around here." she added. "No YaHoo for me tonight, Glen, my mom just asked me to pick up some pie filling on the way home. Mom loves to bake me a cherry pie for Thanksgiving, you know!"

Johna was a striking, charismatic young woman with bright eyes and an enrapturing smile. Her hair was woven into tight, short micro braids. She was outgoing and genuine and put people at ease. While dressed in blue jeans and a sweatshirt, it was easy for Glen to imagine her in uniform leading young Marines into untold danger. She was a natural leader – one of the best to come out of Galesburg, thought Glen, his own two daughters excluded of course.

"How is your family?" Johna asked of Glen.

"Well, I'm fixing to find out tonight after close. Both of my girls are coming home for Thanksgiving, Johna. I haven't seen them for months." Glen volunteered.

As Johna and Glen stood reminiscing about her school exploits, the U.S. withdrawal from Afghanistan and the best type of Thanksgiving pie, a third figure approached the storefront stopping momentarily in the shadow of one of the oak trees to don a black facemask. Unbeknownst to the occupants of the market, they were about to be joined by another whose motives were not so pure and nostalgic. Kyle Bastian, a relatively new resident of Galesburg, was looking for a quick score of cash.

Kyle lived with his elderly mother on South Street in Galesburg, a blighted neighborhood with more Pitbulls than people. A faded confederate flag flew from a makeshift flagpole in the front yard of their small, dilapidated house with a collapsing, one stall, unattached garage. The bushes, volunteer trees and landscaping had grown to envelop the structure. The property did not look out of place in this once proud neighborhood, as most of the homes now had boarded up windows, unmown yards and debris strewn throughout. If you ever needed to buy a demo derby car or a bag of meth, this was your neighborhood.

Johna said, "Well, I'd better get home. Happy Thanksgiving to you and yours, Glen!"

"Same to you, Johna, enjoy that cherry pie." responded Glen.

As Johna pivoted toward the door to make her exit, she caught a glint of polished steel with the peripheral vision of her left eye – a silver 1911 held in the outstretched arm of the most recent person in the store. The gun was pointed at Mr. Kim, and the gunman's hand was shaking noticeably.

"Hands up, Motherfuckers!" bellowed the gunman.

With no time to consider the significance of the threat, Johna instantly and instinctively lunged for the firearm with her left hand and simultaneously swung at the gunman's head with the can of pie filling in her right hand. Having seen the mask-wearing intruder enter the store, Glen had quickly pushed the panic button, reached for the short-barreled shotgun he had long-ago stashed behind the counter and raised it aimed toward the gunman.

The sound of the blast was deafening, ears were ringing, and the odor of spent gunpower pierced the nostrils. The scene seemed to vibrate in a stunned, deadened silence, as a pink mist settled to the tile floor. For that moment in time, all three participants were both alive and dead.

CHAPTER 3

The McClay Family

The sound of laughter could be heard emanating from the home at 121 East Losey Street in Galesburg, as the McClay family joked and kidded one another rolling out pie crust on the huge kitchen's black granite countertops. The McClay home was a veritable fortress of a structure, built in 1928 as a duplex by two sisters who wanted to live together, but separate. It was later converted to a single-family residence and remodeled by a blended family who wanted enough room for all of their five children. The immense house was gorgeous. It sat on two lots. A blond brick with a green tile roof, it was two stories with a full basement for storage. The spacious covered front porch had a ceramic tile floor and allowed the McClays to sit and take in the park-like setting of the neighborhood. It boasted five bedrooms and two full bathrooms upstairs and a master bedroom with en suite on the first floor. Because it had been a duplex, the dining room and kitchen were both double in size, as the center wall of the duplex had divided those rooms in the structure. That center wall had been removed. The kitchen had a full bank of roll out windows facing the north. The dining room had a full bank of windows facing the South toward Losey Street. Two islands in the kitchen and ample counter space, all covered in black granite tops made the kitchen a wonderful place for the family to participate in preparing meals or hosting parties. Gorgeous new glass front cupboards reflected the shimmering light from a large crystal chandelier which descended from the center of the kitchen ceiling. The hand hammered copper farmer's sink was the *coup de grace* for the kitchen's design.

As they waited for Johna to get home from the store, Johna's mother, Jamie, held a clinic on the fine art of making cherry pies for the next days' Thanksgiving dinner. The pumpkin pies were sitting on the counter to cool. Jamie and her husband, Matthew, and their three children, were looking forward to a fun and relaxing Thanksgiving holiday in the family home. Clyde McClay, the couple's oldest son lived in an apartment in town but planned on staying the night Wednesday to help get ready for Thursday's dinner. Matthew was an attorney who practiced law in Knox County and the surrounding west-central Illinois area. Jaimie was a real estate agent but slowed down in her business considerably while her children were young in order to be more engaged with them in their education, extracurricular activities and their upbringing.

Johna's younger brother, Carter, fancied himself the master and challenged his mother to a bake off. A pie aficionado, Carter was generally an all-around good cook and often treated the family to unique and tasty dishes. But when it came to pies, Jamie and Carter were locked in a vicious competition that included regular entries annually at the Knox County Fair. Both had taken home blue ribbons – in alternating years.

Johna's older brother Clyde sat at the island wearing a faded Marine Corps t-shirt nursing a Guinness, the last of a six pack he had brought over with him from his apartment two hours ago. He smiled and took in the banter as the television in the kitchen softly played Hip Hop music at low volume.

"Where the hell is Johna!" asked Clyde. "You sent her to the store an hour ago, Mom."

"You're so impatient, Clyde" Jaimie chided. "Give that girl some space!"

"I haven't spent time with her in months, Mom. Is it too much to ask that she hang out with us for the evening? Damn!" said Clyde.

"She's got a lot on her mind, Clyde. She'll be here soon, I'm sure." Jamie responded. "Your father should be home from work soon, too."

All four knew that Johna was under investigation for an alleged violation of the Uniform Code of Military Justice and a probable war crime arising out of an event which took place two months ago during her last tour in Afghanistan. Extremely embarrassed and full of an overwhelming sense of shame, Johna had confided in each of them that the Marine Corps Judge Advocate General's Office was looking to charge her with an act of extreme cruelty while serving in Afghanistan. She was having trouble sleeping. She was barely eating, and she was experiencing a general sense of depression and anxiety. While there was a scarcity of evidence to support the charge, Johna knew she was guilty and that her fellow marines would eventually give testimony implicating her.

In August, in Kabul, Afghanistan, Second Lieutenant McClay had been present when thirteen U.S. service members were killed and at least eighteen injured in a suicide bomb attack at a Taliban checkpoint outside Hamid Karzai International Airport as the U.S. attempted to airlift the remaining hundreds of Americans and thousands of Afghans who had assisted the U.S. in its war fighting efforts there. Johna and her unit had concluded that the Taliban soldiers manning the checkpoint had been complicit in the bomb attack and must have known the identities of the Islamic State in Khorasan fighters who organized the bombing. In an effort to extract intelligence from one Taliban soldier, Johna used an Afghan translator attached to her unit to interrogate him, and she had tortured the man mercilessly leading to his death. After beating him with the butt of her rifle stock, she had shot him in the leg severing his femoral artery. He bled out.

This fact did not change the way her family felt about Johna. They loved her unconditionally and understood to their cores that she was a deeply moral and decent person. In their view, it was the horror and fog of war that had produced this cruelty, not Johna's heart. That said, although she downplayed it to her family, Johna knew that she would probably be successfully court martialed for the offense.

As Carter swiveled on his stool, he recounted a story about Johna.

"I remember one time when Johna and me were in school, and we were home alone, Johna locked me and Ern in the fenced in dog pen and flung dogshit at us with a broken spatula she found in the yard." Carter sheepishly admitted.

"That is bullshit, Carter! Your sister would never do such a horrible thing! You're making that up." Jaime defended.

"No, mom. I'm serious! Johna kept it up until me and Ern were both gagging and puking." said Carter.

"Well, I don't believe you, Carter. And what kind of a story is that to tell on your sister?" said Jaimie, clearly irritated.

Clyde could barely maintain his composure. He laughed so hard, to his mother's dismay, that he started gasping for air.

"That's enough, boys! We're making pies and we're supposed to be thinking how thankful we are." Jamie scolded.

"You and Ern? Oh my God, Carter. You are killing me." Clyde chortled as he took another drink of his beer.

"You two little fuckers deserved that shit!" laughed Clyde.

Now Carter was laughing uncontrollably as well.

"Alright! That's not true. That's horrible. And that's enough of that talk – both of you." exclaimed Jaimie.

"Of all the stories you could share about your wonderful sister, you have to go and come up with some bullshit like that. What is wrong with you?" Jamie followed.

"Well, she's not perfect, Mom. I know she's your favorite, but …" Carter injected.

"I don't have a favorite! All three of you are my favorites. You are all different, but I love all of you the very same – except you Carter. You are on the shit list right now. You had better get to making some pie crust, boy." Jamie interrupted.

"I'm going to call her." Clyde stated. "I'm starting to get a little worried about her."

CHAPTER 4

Kyle Bastian

The masked gunman attempting to rob Schrodinger's Market, thirty-two-year-old Kyle Bastian, had not been a standout at high School, either athletically or academically. Kyle preferred smoking marijuana with his friends and playing video games into the wee hours of the night on a stolen PS3 gaming system. He was regularly truant from school and didn't finish his senior year. Neither college nor the trades were in Kyle's plan, as he bounced around from one minimum wage job to another and engaged in other inventive ways to acquire the funds necessary to supplement his mother's meager social security check each month. Sullen and sallow, Kyle's pockmarked face was partially covered by a sparce beard and looked like it hadn't seen the light of day for ages. He was thin and wiry and had the bent posture of a much older man. His unlaundered clothes hung on him and wreaked of stale cigarette smoke. It was clear that he did not have a standing appointment with a barber, as his dark hair was long and unkempt. Kyle was nothing to look at.

Kyle's family, the only relatives he was aware

of, consisted of one older half-brother, Mark Downard – currently an inmate at Henry C. Hill Correctional Center in Galesburg, and his seventy-year-old, twice divorced mother, Ardis Bastian, who now suffered from advanced dementia and seemed intent on killing herself by chain-smoking unfiltered Pall Mall cigarettes. Ardis had Kyle later in life when she was 38 years old.

While Ardis would have qualified for Medicaid assistance to fund a long-term care facility, she was a retired CNA who had worked at one of the nursing homes in Chicago for long enough to know that she preferred to attempt to live on her own with her cats and son in the small, run down South Street house she called home. She also felt a responsibility to look after her adult son, Kyle, who, despite being able-bodied, proved incapable of self-support. Ardis dreaded the notion that Kyle would join Mark in prison and felt that she had failed both children while doing her best to raise the boys as a single mother working full time.

Ardis and Kyle were hoarders. Their small house belied the sheer volumes of molding trash, soiled clothing, dirty dishes, urine-soaked stacks of old newspapers and dried cat feces contained within it. Frankly, the roof was in such a state of disrepair that it was probably held up largely by the mounds of garbage. The rancid smell of mildew and excrement mixed with cigarette smoke deterred even the most loyal of friends from setting foot in the house. The kitchen was so filled with empty pizza boxes, dirty dishes and fast-food bags that it was unusable. Other than a narrow path to the refrigerator door, the rest of the kitchen was essentially off limits. Both Ardis and Kyle slept in the living room with the cats, the television and the video game console. Ardis slept on the couch and Kyle slept in a tattered old recliner.

"Kyle is going to take me to Perkin's for Thanksgiving dinner tomorrow," Ardis bragged to her neighbor Mary on her Obama phone. "Kyle has been saving his money and promised to treat me to turkey and the fixings." She added, as she took a sip from her cold cup of coffee.

"That's wonderful, Ardis! What a thoughtful son you have." replied Mary as she rolled her eyes in utter disgust. The idea that Kyle was doing anything for his mother stretched the bounds of credulity for Mary, who had lived next door to the Bastians for several years. Mary was suspicious that Kyle had been pilfering his mother's social security income to support his lifestyle of sloth, fast food and substance abuse. But she didn't have the heart or the gumption to turn the matter over to the authorities to investigate for exploitation. Instead, she provided what assistance she could to Ardis, making sure she had what she needed, her garbage cans were placed on the curb on Thursdays, and that she was reminded of her doctor's appointments. She was also a listening ear.

"What is Kyle up to these days, Ardis?" Mary inquired feigning interest.

"I don't recall." Ardis mumbled, her cigarette dangling from her mouth. "I think he still works part time doing something for. . . I'm not sure. Darn this brain, Mary! I just get so confused sometimes."

"That's okay, Ardis. I understand. The last I knew Kyle was working at Farm King." said Mary, attempting to fill in the gaps in Ardis's memory.

"You're right. That's it ... I think." Ardis responded untruthfully. "He's so good to me." Ardis continued trying to change the subject away from a fact-based discussion.

"Well, it's getting late, Ardis. I had better let you go. I'm sure Kyle will be coming home soon." said Mary.

As the two hung up, Mary realized that they never seemed to discuss Mark. That subject was simply off limits. It was as though Mark had passed away or never existed. Whether Ardis had forgotten about Mark or she was so disturbed and embarrassed by his incarceration, the subject was never broached. The only thing Ardis ever wanted to talk about was Kyle, her cats and what she could remember about what CNN was reporting on television.

According to Mary's internet research, and the rumors she had been able to glean from the neighborhood, Mark had been convicted of murder in a gang-related shooting on the South Side of Chicago years ago. The Bastians had moved to Galesburg from Chicago to be closer to Mark, but the relationship had soured, and neither Kyle nor Ardis visited the prison or corresponded with Mark anymore. They had lived on South Street by Mary for five years and had done absolutely nothing to improve the appearance of the property, unless you consider broken down lawn-mowers and year-round Christmas lights to be art.

Kyle had also had several brushes with the law himself. The Galesburg Police Department was a regular visitor to the house at 1021 West South Street. Most notably, Kyle had been a key suspect in a spate of car and house burglaries throughout the more patrician neighborhoods in the north end of town. Nobody was ever charged with those crimes, but Kyle and one of his friends had been brought in several times for questioning, and a search warrant had been executed on the South Street house looking for stolen purses, car stereos and the like. It was hard to imagine the disgusting job of rummaging through the debris-filled home looking for stolen goods. Maybe that would make a good episode of "Dirty Jobs" with Mike Rowe, thought Mary. Nothing had even been found except Kyle's stash of grotesque pornography.

Kyle's closest call with the law involved an altercation in a bar six months ago in which Kyle had been attacked and beaten mercilessly by an intoxicated patron. Thin-skinned and quick to anger, Kyle had smarted off to the man, calling him a douchebag and thereby provoking the large middle-aged truck driver to leap from his bar stool, tackle Kyle and punch his face repeatedly. Kyle, small in stature but innovative and scrappy, had been able to extricate himself from the drunk man's hold and grab a pool cue sitting on a nearby pool table. Once both men were on their feet, Kyle broke the cue in two and ran it through his assailant's abdomen putting an end to the fracas. It also put an end to the man's life, as he bled out on the floor before help could arrive. Kyle fled the scene after the bartender called the police and ambulance.

When the police finally caught up with Kyle early the next morning, Officer Kolby Franklin arrested him and he was charged by the State with first degree murder, with bond set at one million dollars, ten percent to apply. Obviously, Kyle did not have a hundred thousand dollars to bond out of jail, but he did have Matthew McClay, a reputable criminal defense lawyer who upon reading of Kyle's case in the newspaper volunteered to represent Kyle pro bono. Surely, thought Mr. McClay, Kyle would be seen as having acted with legal justification in defending himself against an attack by a larger man. Yes, he had to contend with the fact that Kyle had provoked the attack with name-calling, but that was no hill for a climber. And Matthew was correct. Leveraging his close relationship with the Knox County State's Attorney, Matthew was quickly able to convince him to reduce the charge to a misdemeanor of disorderly conduct, to which Kyle pled guilty. With time served, Kyle paid only a small fine plus court costs, and was placed on court supervision for a period of one year, after the successful completion of which the charge would be dropped. Kyle spent only a few weeks in pretrial detainment over the event and had incurred no attorney's fees. Matthew McClay had advised Kyle that this was his second chance in life, something most people don't get. And he implored Kyle not to squander it, but instead, to turn his life around and make something of himself.

Not to be outdone by his half-brother, Mark, Kyle had also acquired a handgun during one of his burglary sprees. A stainless-steel Remington 1911 chambered in .45 caliber, the semiautomatic pistol was Kyle's pride and joy, and following his recent entanglement with the justice system over a bar fight, he also considered it his equalizer. Kyle vowed never to be the victim again. He would never have been able to afford such a weapon. Retailing for more than $1,000, it had surely been prized by its rightful owner. While he was disposed to brandish the weapon in front of his friends and occasionally to impress the girls, Kyle was very careful about where he kept the gun. He hid it every night – along with one full magazine of hollow point ammunition -- wrapped in an oil-soaked rag inside a large plastic baggie under a disabled riding lawnmower in the largely inaccessible back yard. Kyle felt safer with his 1911. He regularly regaled his small cohort of Galesburg friends with tall tales of growing up on the south side of Chicago. He fancied himself a tough guy, but he was really just a mouthy sissy who couldn't beat his way out of a wet paper bag.

CHAPTER 5

The Kim Family

Glen Kim was a fortunate man. He had a beautiful wife and two stunning daughters. His wife, Lin, was a first generation American of Korean descent. Her parents had emigrated from South Korea in the 1960s and Lin was born in Oakland, California in 1962. She was 10 years younger than Glen. Lin had grown up in California and attended the University of California at Berkley where she studied art and focused in oil painting. She met Glen in the 1980s in Galesburg, Illinois of all places, when she was a visiting resident artist at a program sponsored by the Galesburg Community Art Center attracting artists from all over the country. Lin stayed in Galesburg where she later assumed the leadership of the not-for-profit Art Center and served as an adjunct instructor at Knox College in the fine arts department. She and Glen married in 1988 and soon thereafter had their two daughters, Park and Yun, in rapid succession. Even though Lin was busy with her work at the Art Center and the college, she always found time to lend a hand to Glen at the market, and Park and Yun were usually in tow. Somehow, she also found time to paint. To the extent the interior of Schrodinger's Market could be considered stylish, that was Lin's contribution. She had a keen eye for design and all things aesthetic, and very few things in Glen's life escaped that influence.

Park and Yun were two years apart in age but couldn't be more different in personality. Both were slight of build and inherited their mother's beauty. But the similarities stopped there. Park was a well-behaved, studious child who performed well in school and always wanted to please her parents. Yun wasn't. Its fair to say that Yun didn't want to be in her older sister's shadow and struck out in her own direction. Innately intelligent, Yun didn't apply herself in the traditional ways. Her schoolwork was mediocre, and it was not unusual for her mother to find that Yun had hidden or destroyed a disciplinary note sent home from the teacher. Yun had a flair for the dramatic. She read with great passion and acted out her favorite scenes in literature for her family at mealtimes. She became heavily involved in school and community theater productions and went on to major in theater at Knox College. Park, too, attended Knox College, but her focus was mathematics. It was her goal to become an actuary or a math professor. Neither Glen nor Lin had a mathematical bone in their body, except that Glen was quite adept at the basic math necessary to successfully manage his business.

Unfortunately, Knox College was tightening its belt and did away with its employee perquisite of tuition-free education for children of adjunct instructors. Nevertheless, through tremendous financial aid from the college, together with numerous local scholarships, the girls were able to attend Knox despite their parent's relatively impecunious financial condition.

And their first-class liberal arts educations allowed them to flourish in their lives and careers. Park continued her studies at Northwestern University in Evanston where she earned a Ph.D. and took a position as an associate professor of mathematics at the University of Chicago in Hyde Park. She married an investment banker at Merill Lynch, and the couple resided in Chicago. Yun married a wealthy commodities trader on the Chicago Board of Trade and continued her career as a professional actress, regularly appearing in plays and productions in Chicago.

Both Park and Yun and their husbands travelled to Galesburg to spend Wednesday night with Glen and Lin for Thanksgiving. The Kims lived in a modest three-bedroom bungalow on North Cherry Street in Galesburg. The home and garden were immaculate – everything in its place. The interior walls were adorned with many of Lin's paintings, the ones she couldn't stand to part with, and the ones nobody wanted. Her colorful frescos seemed to define the space in each room with blues, reds and yellows. Furnished in a minimalist theme, the living room and dining rooms were adequate in size and relatively uncluttered. The kitchen was small but well-appointed and very utilitarian. One bedroom down and two up, there would be just enough room to accommodate the family overnight. A single, downstairs bathroom had been the source of many disputes as the girls grew up. But the three-season room on the back of the house facing the garden is where the action was. It was like a screened in porch on steroids. Comfortable and spacious, the room included a woodburning fireplace, overstuffed leather chairs and a couch. This was the room where everyone gathered. This was where Yun acted out her dramas for her adoring family audience. This was where the six family members imagine spending Wednesday night catching up with each other and recounting childhood stories.

Glen usually made it home from his market by six o'clock p.m. every night, when he turns the store over to Josh Hernandez to work until close at ten. Tonight, however, Glen planned to close early at six, so he and Josh could spend time with family for the holidays. Glen was also very cognizant of the dangers that attend nights like this. He had personal experience with the realities of clerking a convenience market at night, especially one in a depressed town and located on a state highway going through it.

In fact, Glen had personally been robbed in the store three times. Ten years ago, one of his clerks, Scott Morrissey, was shot to death by someone robbing the store after Glen had left Scott to close. The perpetrator of that crime was never found and brought to justice. Glen was devastated at the loss of his young friend and employee. Glen had considered allowing Scott to buy into the business as part of his succession plan, just as Mr. Colton had done for Glen. But Glen had not broached the subject with Scott, and the plan still resided only in Glen's memory and his attorney's files. This experience scarred Glen deeply.

These incidents had hardened Glen considerably. So much so that Glen relished the notion that someone would try to rob him again. He fashioned himself a vigilante in its truest sense. He actually fantasized about it and acted out how he would react when it happened. It was as though Glen hoped that the man who shot Scott would attempt to strike again. He was prepared for the firefight, both mentally and physically. He regularly went to the local gun range in nearby Monmouth, Illinois to practice his technique, and he obsessed over the question of what gun or guns he should arm himself with at the store. For the time being, Glen had settled on a single barreled pump action twelve-gauge shotgun loaded with five, three-inch rounds of buckshot. It was manufactured by Mossberg with a short barrel and a pistol-type grip. Marketed as the Mossberg 590 Shockwave, it was a modern blunderbuss, and it was hard to believe it was legal. He stored it well within reach as he was behind the counter. Glen also carried concealed, while he was in the store and otherwise.

Glen was drawing up construction plans for building a secret gunroom in the basement of his home to store and display all of his guns, from Arisakas and Mosin-Nagants to hunting rifles and shotguns. His collection of AR-15s, AR-10s, an AR-9 and an AK 47 was impressive. He also owned a handful of pistols in several calibers, some revolvers and some semiautomatic. Presently these weapons resided in multiple gun safes, but Glen would have prefered to have them mounted on the walls of a dedicated gun room housing all of his ammunition and gear. This, in Glen's mind, required either a steel reinforced door or even better a hidden door incorporated into another feature of the house, like a bookshelf.

Most people were unaware of Glen's attitude or thought processes in this connection. It was not something Glen shared with anyone but his wife and his attorney. Glen knew that people tend to be afraid of guns, and people like him with massive quantities of ammunition and firearms were considered "gun nuts". But Glen was bound and determined to be ready for a fight. The police had never given Glen a sense of protection and safety. Maybe it was the fact that they never caught the man who shot Scott, but it probably went deeper than that.

As a young Korean boy, Glen had been the victim of bullying and incessant racist jokes by kids of all races and backgrounds. He had been taunted and teased about his ethnicity and constantly called names by ignoramuses who had never been out of Galesburg. He was not a strong boy nor particularly physically fit. He lost every fight he entered. He was never protected by the police or anyone else for that matter. He just picked himself up and dusted himself off and went about his day.

Not long after Glen started working at Schrodinger's Market, racist graffiti started showing up on the exterior walls. Someone had spray-painted swastikas on the bricks, and Glen had the responsibility of cleaning it off. Mr. Colton never let that kind of thing stand. Law enforcement did absolutely nothing about it, nor could they, realistically. It was unclear what the motivation for the graffiti had been. Was Glen the target, or did someone believe the name Schrodinger sounded Jewish? It was impossible to tell, and in Galesburg the local hoodlums were such ignorant miscreants that there may have been no discernable meaning whatsoever. However, those things stuck with Glen as he grew up and had a family, and it caused him to not rely on law enforcement.

But Glen loved his community and he felt strongly it was his duty to give back to his community in exchange for the living it had provided he and his wife over the years. Mr. Colton had been an extremely generous mentor to Glen, and Glen did the same for other community youth in part by volunteering as a little league baseball coach. Having two girls, Glen enjoyed the time and comradery with the young men and boys who coached and played in the league. He coached for years until Scott was killed in the market robbery. That tragic episode caused Glen to withdraw into himself and abandon most of his community volunteerism.

CHAPTER 6

The Police Officer

Officer Kolby Franklin was a new hire to the Galesburg Police Department. With low seniority, it was Officer Franklin who pulled the second shift (5 p.m. to midnight) as a patrolman on Wednesday, November 24, the night before Thanksgiving. Kolby had graduated at the top his class at nearby Knoxville High School and maintained a 4.0 grade point average at Western Illinois University in its law enforcement program. A standout at the police academy, Galesburg was eager to add Kolby to its ranks.

Naturally gifted at math, Kolby had always had an interest in quantum mechanics and had taken classes in the field as electives. He also indulged that interest by continuing to read extensively on the subject after graduation. He loved to muse over the various laws and theories that describe the behavior of subatomic particles and how those behaviors could seem to violate existing physical laws. By contrast, Kolby was also very interested in enforcing the criminal laws which seemed a much more concrete and practical application of his efforts. Asked in his interview why he wanted to be a police officer, Kolby had answered that he liked to solve puzzles and help people. His mind was always working. He read the paper every morning and played the sudoku puzzles at every opportunity. He loved to tease and entertain his fellow officers in the break room with the seemingly ridiculous lessons from quantum mechanics.

"What if the law of local causality is false?" he had asked the officers assembled in the breakroom.

"What in the fuck are you talking about, Franklin?" was the reply from Officer Johnson.

"You know – every change in nature is produced by some cause, and an object is directly influenced only by its immediate surroundings. What if that is false?" said Kolby.

"What does that have to do with anything in my life?" asked Officer Johnson.

"What would it mean for the criminal justice system if we took quantum theory seriously? What if I could prove that a person can be in two places at the same time? What if I could prove that events can be caused by something distant and unseen?" asked Kolby.

"You'd be a helluva defense lawyer if you could prove all that, man." scoffed Officer Johnson.

"That's what I'm getting at, Johnson!" Kolby exclaimed, as Officer Johnson grumbled, called Kolby a douchebag under his breath and took his coffee out of the break room followed by the rest of the group.

He is also drawn to baseball where he had excelled on the field as a boy and now has an encyclopedic knowledge of the Major League Baseball statistics and sabermetrics. He is a long-standing fan of the Chicago Cubs – who would have done well to hire him as an analyst. The other officers much preferred to talk baseball with him.

An hour into his shift that night, as he was patrolling downtown Galesburg in his blue and white police cruiser, Officer Franklin got a call on his radio that the alarm had been triggered at Schrodinger's Market on Main Street. He noted the time – 6:05 p.m. -- acknowledged the dispatch and proceeded hastily toward the Market with the idea that there might be a robbery in progress.

Kolby was quite familiar with Schrodinger's Market. Growing up, he had frequented the market. Knoxville was such a small, sleepy town, all of the Knoxville kids would drive or bum rides to Galesburg for excitement and something to do. The police in Knoxville regularly hassled the kids in town, and that also served to drive them to neighboring Galesburg. Some kids would even walk or ride their bikes the considerable distance. The adventure often included a trip to Schrodinger's for a snack. For Kolby, it also meant an opportunity to visit with his little league baseball coach, Glen Kim. Kolby and Park Kim had both attended math classes at the "College for Kids" program at Knox College growing up. They even dated briefly, but the inter-town rivalry proved too much for the budding relationship. They remained friends and kept track of each other through college and into their careers. But Kolby got a huge kick out of visiting with Glen, and the converse was true as well. Kolby would regale Glen with baseball stories and statistics, and Glen would share with Kolby what it was like growing up as an orphaned immigrant. Of course, Kolby would inquire about Park's exploits and Glen was always proud to update him. Kolby's friends would often have to pull him out of the market to continue their adventure in Galesburg.

As he approached the market, Officer Franklin began to analyze what he might find. He speculated that Glen Kim was likely minding the store. He expected there to be at least one person attempting to rob the store. And he wondered how many, if any, other patrons might be in the store. As he arrived and exited his vehicle, he could make out what from a distance appeared to be three bodies: Two bodies were lying on the floor near the exit, and a third body appeared to be slumped over the counter. He briefly hesitated before attempting to enter the store to call for backup. He drew his service weapon, a Glock 22 in .40 caliber, and proceeded closer to the glass front door to gain a better vantage point. The leaves crackled under his footsteps, and his body camera captured the steam from his breath as he knelt beside the door. His adrenaline was high.

In this stressful moment, Officer Franklin was instantly reminded of his studies of quantum mechanics and how it was possible that until he opened the door to fully observe the scene the occupants of Schrodinger's Market could be both alive and dead at the same time. The quantum system, he thought, remains in a superposition until it reacts with or is observed by the external world.

As he waited for his backup to arrive, Kolby peered into the store through the plate glass window. The glass on the front door had been shattered. He recognized his friend and baseball coach, Glen, and he also recognized Kyle as the kid he had arrested as a murder suspect several months before. Finally, he thought he recognized the third body as Johna McClay, the local semi-celebrity who had made a name for herself in Galesburg, both athletically and scholastically. Her father had successfully represented Kyle on the murder charge. Kyle's ski mask had been pulled to the top of his head, with his face fully exposed and facing the front door, and Johna was draped over Kyle's body.

Whatever had happened, it appeared to be over. There was no need or justification for Officer Franklin to rush in. He hoped with all his might that his eyes deceived him. Why is it taking so long for his back up to arrive? The police station was only a block away off the square. He wondered if it would all go away if he just didn't open that door.

His thoughts were interrupted by the wailing siren of an approaching police car, and he reverted to his training. He immediately radioed dispatch for EMS. In his mind he made a split-second calculation:

There were eight potential outcomes here. They could all be alive. They could all be dead. Glen could be the only one alive. Johna could be the only one alive. Kyle could be the only one alive. Glen could be the only one dead. Johna could be the only one dead. Kyle could be the only one dead.

"We have three down." He informed the dispatcher. The structure of the store was like the steel chamber into which Erwin Schrodinger's theoretical cat had been placed along with a tiny bit of radioactive matter. In the thought experiment posed by Erwin Schrodinger, designed to debunk a certain view of quantum theory, a paradox is created. If one of the atoms decays while the cat is in the box, the cat is killed by a mechanism. If, as is equally probable, none of the atoms decay in that timeframe, the cat stays alive. Before the box is opened to see the result, the cat is in "superposition", both dead and alive at the same time. Albert Einstein praised Schrodinger's thought experiment for its ability to disclose the absurdity of the theory. He wrote to Schrodinger stating in part, "Nobody really doubts that the presence or absence of the cat is something independent of the act of observation."

Just then, a third police cruiser pull up to the store and came to an abrupt stop. Backup had arrived. It was time to enter the market.

CHAPTER 7

Matthew McClay

Matthew McClay, while a little bit late, did arrive home at approximately 6:10 p.m. After leaving his law office later than he planned, he had also been slowed down by an ambulance and two police cars responding to some situation near the square. His week was over, and he was looking forward to spending the next four days at home with family. He felt blessed to have his lovely wife and three successful children, none of whom had needed his pro bono services as an attorney. He zipped into the large, detached garage in his BMW X5 and parked next to Jamie's Jaguar F type sports car. He locked the doors and jogged into the house as the garage door creaked to a close.

Once in the kitchen, he was welcomed home in unison by his sons.

"Dad!" they shouted, as Matthew put his overcoat coat in the closet and loosened his necktie. "How was your day?"

His day had actually been disturbing, as his last client appointment of the day had been a woman seeking Matthew's representation in a what appeared to be a contentious divorce case. Most divorce cases left Matthew feeling dirty, like he needed to go home and take a shower. They involved dealing closely with hurt, angry and vulnerable people at their very worst. This one looked to be no different. His client was having a secret affair with her husband's medical practice partner, but she wanted to make sure she was still going to receive a large award of property and alimony in the divorce she wanted to file. The minor children seemed to be much less of a focus for her.

"Excellent!" he replied. "But I'm glad to be home."

"We're just making pies with mom and waiting for Johna to get home" said Carter.

"Oh, I smelled pumpkin pie cooking as I walked up the driveway, Carter" said Matthew.

"Those are done, dad. They're just cooling now. We are working on Cherry pies now." explained Carter. "We're waiting for Johna to bring us some more pie filling."

"What's up, old man?" asked Clyde.

"Clyde, you know how I hate it when you refer to me as 'old man.'" retorted Matthew.

"I'm just kidding you, Pops. I'm glad to see you." answered Clyde.

As Matthew invaded the refrigerator for a beer, he was happy to locate a lone Heffeweizen way in the back.

"I'm glad nobody else likes my Heffeweizen . . . Clyde." Matthew said, sarcastically.

"I brought my own beer tonight, Pops. I came prepared." said Clyde.

"Oh really? Did you bring any for me to replenish my supply after you decimated it last weekend?" asked Matthew.

"I'm sorry. I figured it being Thanksgiving and all that you'd have a stocked fridge." said Clyde.

"I'll take a beer, Dad?" offered Carter, only half joking.

"Fat chance, Carter! You stay out of the sauce young man." was Matthew's stern reply.

"Yeah, you little booger." Jaimie piped in. "He's been telling ridiculous stories about his sister all evening, Honey."

"We need to talk about Kevin!" joked Clyde, referring to the movie.

"Cool it, butthole!" yelled Carter.

"Boys! That's enough!" Jaime scolded.

Matthew sat down on a stool next to where Jaimie was standing at the counter cooking and wrapped his arm around her waist. Sipping his beer, Matthew recounted the ins and outs of his day, always being careful to protect privileged and confidential information. It is difficult for an attorney to fully vent to his wife and family about the things that got under his skin at work. So much of what he does is off limits due to the rules of professional responsibility that limit what he can disclose. That can negatively affect the relationship, especially between husband and wife, as the two are prohibited from sharing freely certain thoughts, fears, anxieties and triumphs. Few things are worse than not being able to share with your spouse a significant victory you had in a case you are handling, or a horrible client secret shared with you, as that type of information is often protected as confidential. Any disclosure of the information can lead to liability and even sanction or disbarment.

"Practicing law sure is a weird way to make a living." quipped Matthew intending to get a responsive question out of Jamie.

"Why's that, Honey?" Jamie played along.

"Well, I feel like I'm fighting my own clients sometimes, in addition to fighting the other side and fighting the judge. Some of the best lawyering I do is getting my client to agree to take my advice." responded Matthew. "I feel like I'm constantly fighting everyone. I just want to jump off the ride sometimes."

"Quit your whining! You have the next four days to relax and recharge your batteries, Matthew. It's going to be wonderful to enjoy each other's company and catch up with Johna." said Jaimie.

"Yeah, Dad. I'll trade you jobs." Clyde chimed in. "You can work for the City street department, outside in the elements fixing water main breaks at twenty below zero while I wear a suit and tie and sit in the warm, comfortable office all day."

Matthew gave Clyde a long cold stare with a furled brow. "Careful, smartass. I might be inclined to take you up on that offer." Matthew responded in jest.

"Johna's not answering her phone." said Clyde anxiously as he raised his phone to dial her number again.

Then there was a knock on the front door.

CHAPTER 8

Wednesday Night at the Kims'

The Kim household was starting to fill up. Lin was home in the kitchen, and the girls and their husbands had both arrived and were upstairs putting their luggage away and bantering with each other. For both of their husbands, this was the first time they had all been together in the Kim home. Glen and Lin had asked Josh if he would like to join them for Thanksgiving dinner, but he had politely declined stating that he had plans to spend the holiday with his girlfriend in Carbondale.

The girls' rooms upstairs were nicely decorated, but both still exhibited some evidence that a teenage girl had once lived there. This allowed for a great deal of teasing and laughter.

Lin yelled upstairs, "Come on down and join me, you guys!"

"We'll all be down in a minute, Mom. We're looking through our high school yearbooks." Park responded.

"Bring them down." Lin said.

All four came downstairs, navigating the staircase while looking at the yearbooks and laughing.

"Who is *that*? Park asked Yun, pointing at a photo of Yun from a high school production of West Side Story.

Yun's husband, Ian, focused on the image intently.

"You played the role of Maria in West Side Story?" asked Ian proudly.

"I did." Replied Yun. "And guess who played Tony." Yun teased.

"Let me guess … Brian Gathof, your high school boyfriend?" Ian proffered with a tinge of jealousy.

"You know it!" Park exclaimed. "But that relationship was doomed."

"Lucky for me!" said Ian, as the four plopped down into the overstuffed leather furniture on the back porch.

Park's husband, John laughed and continued the torture of Ian.

From the kitchen, Lin brought a pitcher of homemade egg nog onto the porch, spiked with a goodly amount of rum, of course. The pitcher was accompanied by six leaded crystal glasses. A platter of Buckeyes and chocolate fudge sat tantalizingly on the coffee table, and Park's husband, John, looked like he might be interested in sampling them.

"Help yourselves." Lin suggested as she pointed at the table. "Glen will be home any minute."

And there was no hesitation as the five of them dug right in. All were looking forward to Glen getting home to join the festivities, but there was great food and drink to be had. For the moment, the high school yearbooks played second fiddle to the egg nog and candy.

Then there was a knock on the front door.

CHAPTER 9

Wednesday Night at the Bastian Home

It seemed like any other night at the Bastian house. Ardis sat on the couch watching CNN, smoking cigarettes and drinking cold coffee. The sound on the television could be heard down the street despite the fact that Ardis was sitting within just a few feet of the old Phillips set. Ardis was waiting for Kyle to get home so the two could figure out what to order for dinner. She had just hung up from her call with her friend and neighbor, Mary Carlson.

CNN's Anderson Cooper was holding court in the cramped Bastian living room, telling the nation – or what small fraction of it still watched CNN – that "Let's Go Brandon" was hate speech and should subject people saying it to punishment. Ardis agreed. She couldn't recall what "Let's Go Brandon" meant, but she generally agreed with everything Anderson Cooper had to say, despite that it might eviscerate the First Amendment. Mary Carlson, on the other hand, was a Fox News viewer, and the two did not see eye to eye politically. Nevertheless, they remained friends, and Mary knew enough never to contradict Ardis - even when she said up was down. You learn that pretty quickly when you spend any time with someone with Alzheimer's Disease. While Ardis loved to watch Anderson Cooper, she was just biding her time for Chris Cuomo's show. Ardis thought he was handsome and liked how he sounded -- again, something that she and Mary would have to agree to disagree upon. Ardis knew that she had to get her CNN watching in quickly before Kyle got home and commandeered the television for videogaming purposes. But this night proved to be different, as Kyle didn't venture home as he usually did for an evening of fast food and gaming.

Then there was a knock on the front door.

CHAPTER 10

The Aftermath

The hardest part of the job is informing the next of kin that their loved one has passed, thought Officer Franklin. Almost as hard, is the task of informing someone that their loved one had been gravely injured and taken to the hospital. He put on his game face, reminded himself of this police training, and he entered the store with two officers right behind him.

Glen Kim had installed video surveillance cameras throughout Schrodinger's Market immediately after Scott was killed in a store robbery. Those cameras were key to understanding exactly what had occurred in the market the evening of November 24. That footage, coupled with the forensic evidence, would show that Kyle shot Glen as Johna lunged for him. Johna knocked Kyle unconscious with the pie filling can. And Johna had inadvertently stepped into the path of Glen's shotgun blast shielding Kyle and causing the shot pellets to enter her upper back and head killing her instantly. Glen, while seriously wounded with a single gunshot, was still alive. So was Kyle.

The Galesburg Police Department sent officers to each of the three homes to notify the families of what had befallen their loved ones and where they had been sent – Johna to the city morgue, Kyle to Galesburg Cottage Hospital Emergency Room and Glen to St. Mary Medical Center Emergency Room in Galesburg. Each of the three officers spent the time necessary with the family to which they were assigned to carefully and compassionately explain what had happened, as best as could be discerned. This holiday season wasn't going to go as planned for any of the three families.

In a way, the McClays had mentally prepared themselves for that knock on the door. They understood that Johna was often in harm's way as an active member of the armed services. They didn't expect it to come from the Galesburg Police Department at a time when Johna was home on leave. They were devastated.

Ardis Bastian immediately called Mary Carlson who quickly volunteered to drive Ardis to the hospital where Kyle had regained consciousness but showed signs of a severe concussion. He would need an MRI. Ardis was scared and embarrassed in equal parts. How could this have happened to her son, and how could her son have done this to someone? A police officer was positioned outside of the door of Kyle's hospital room, as Kyle was under arrest for, among other charges, felony murder. Johna's death occurring during the course of Kyle's commission of a felony – armed robbery – would support the charge. Kyle would later be diagnosed with a skull fracture and concussion but would make a full recovery after treatment. Matthew McClay would certainly not be representing Kyle pro bono on these charges, and after pleading not guilty Kyle would sit in pretrial detention for a very long time.

The Kim family rushed to St. Mary's hospital to see Glen before he was taken into the operating room for emergency surgery. The .45 caliber round had entered his chest cavity, missing his heart and spine but severely damaging a lung, and he had a sucking chest wound. The five of them got a look at Glen as he was wheeled into surgery. Glen's worried eyes met their gaze, but no words were exchanged. They camped out in the waiting room nervously awaiting news from the surgeon. The excitement of the evening had turned to dread. The Knox County State's Attorney had determined that no arrest warrant would be sought for Glen arising out of the shooting. It appeared clear that Glen had been acting in self-defense, and the killing of Johna by Glen had been a tragic accident. No criminal charges would ever be filed against Glen by the State. Glen would survive his injury. But this episode in Glen's life was not over by any stretch of the imagination.

Matthew McClay, alone, went to the city morgue to identify his daughter – a task so excruciating that he would not have wished it on his worst enemy. He broke down upon seeing her body and was glad he had not allowed Jamie to accompany him. The rest of the McClay family sat in their home, stunned and silent in unaccepting disbelief.

Matthew wanted justice, and he did not believe that Kyle's arrest and criminal prosecution was satisfactory. Matthew's friendly relationship with the State's Attorney came to an abrupt end when he declined to accede to Matthew's request that Glen be prosecuted as well. Matthew wanted Glen to pay for having ended his precious daughter's life. If the State's Attorney wasn't going to prosecute Glen, then Matthew would bring a wrongful death lawsuit against Glen in civil court and bankrupt him.

For most of the rest of the community, the evening went on as usual. But for these three families nothing would ever be the same.

CHAPTER 11

Johna McClay's Funeral

Five days later, Johna McClay's visitation was held at the Hutchison, Peterson and Wilson funeral home in Galesburg. As with many such services for young decedents, the number of people who attended Johna's visitation and funeral was overwhelming. Members of Matthew's family, as well as members of Jamie's family, were in attendance. Matthew, Jamie, Clyde and Carter stood in the receiving line for hours as Johna's friends, neighbors, former teammates, classmates, coaches, teachers, acquaintances and family friends filed through to pay their respects and get closure.

Among those family friends was one of Matthew's colleagues, Larry Minor. Larry hugged each of the family members and then expressed his profound sorrow and condolences to Matthew.

"Matthew, I cannot imagine the grief you must be experiencing right now. To lose a child, and one as exceptional as Johna ... there are no words." said Larry.

"Larry, we certainly appreciate you coming. We need all the support and well-wishes we can get.

This is no doubt the most excruciating thing I have ever experienced, and I am just so worried about Jamie, Clyde and Carter and how they're going to deal with it." said Matthew fighting back the tears.

"God will never give you more than you can handle, Matthew." said Larry.

Matthew was not a religious man, and that didn't comfort him. He didn't believe that Johna was in a better place. He didn't believe he would ever get over the intense sense of loss. He felt that he had nothing.

Johna's funeral was graveside at East Linwood Cemetery in Galesburg as a cold wind whipped across the open landscape. She was afforded full military honors. The funeral procession seemed like it had been a mile long and was escorted by officers from the Galesburg Police Department. The line of cars with their headlights on were met by traffic pulled over to the side of the road in observance of the procession. It was an unusually cold day, with temperatures dipping under 20 degrees. The service was mercifully short. It was not very religious. The Marine Corps presented Jamie McClay with a folded American flag. Even the warmly clad mourners were shivering as they looked on somberly at the casket being lowered into the earth. It just seemed like such an unimaginable waste of a human life.

CHAPTER 12

The Bastian Trial

Kyle Bastian's criminal trial was delayed for many months by the defense over concerns Kyle was not competent to assist in his own defense. Kyle's public defender filed a motion suggesting that Kyle's head injury left him in a condition where he was unable to recall the facts surrounding the crime alleged. After a State psychiatrist examined Kyle and found him to be manufacturing his amnesia, Kyle's trial was relatively short and noncontroversial. His public defender didn't have much to work with. Glen had testified and laid an evidentiary foundation for introduction of the videotape footage of the crime. "The videotape" doesn't lie" argued the prosecutor.

According to Illinois law, "A person who kills an individual without lawful justification commits first degree murder if, in performing the acts which cause the death...he or she is attempting or committing a forcible felony other than second degree murder."

As Kyle sat silent at counsel table with his attorney, he felt a deep sense of despair because he knew he was going to prison for a long time. But he felt even worse that his actions had destroyed the life of

Matthew McClay, the only person in his life who had shown him such altruistic kindness. Had he heeded Mr. McClay's advice and set himself straight, this wouldn't have happened.

The jury took less than two hours to return a guilty verdict on all counts, including felony murder in the first degree.

Kyle's presentence report was for the most part unremarkable with the exception of his disorderly conduct charge that had involved the death of another man. The victim impact statements at his sentencing were extremely powerful, and the words of Matthew McClay were an eloquent and moving eulogy of his daughter and oblique condemnation of the defendant. Weighing the statutory factors, the trial judge concluded that a lengthy sentence of forty years in prison was appropriate. Of course, under Illinois law regarding truth in sentencing, Kyle would likely serve one hundred percent of that sentence, without "good time" reductions in his sentence. The sentence was harsh, and it probably didn't hurt that Matthew McClay had practiced law in the same judicial circuit with the trial judge for thirty years.

The media had taken more than a passing interest in the case. Murders were not common in Knox County. At least they hadn't been until the last few years. This story had all of the usual components, but it also included a defendant who had been successfully defended in a previous murder case by the father of the victim in this case. That irony was not lost on the local newspaper reporters or their editors eager to revive their relevance. The local radio stations were reporting regularly on the story. The area television news outlets sent their reporters and trucks down to Galesburg from Peoria and the Quad Cities for the obligatory thirty-second sound bite on the evening news a few times. No one close to the case, or who had a clue as to the pertinent facts, would consent to an interview, but that didn't stop the media from airing a statement from the Bastian's bathrobe-clad neighbor who had apparently neglected to grab his dentures but who was more than happy to give his take on the matter. A homeless woman in the downtown area was also interviewed about Schrodinger's Market and what had happened that fateful night. The reporting was fairly typical and mostly accurate, but several of the news stories focused on and appeared to criticize Matthew McClay for his role in allowing Kyle Bastian to be free to commit this awful crime. Criminal defense lawyers get a bad rap, generally. But the schadenfreude associated with this reporting was palpable and disturbing. Of course, the irony was not lost on Matthew either, and the idea that his actions in that regard had likely contributed to his own daughter's death burned a hole into his soul. No good deed goes unpunished.

CHAPTER 13

The Civil Suit

One year and 364 days following Johna's death, Matthew McClay filed suit against Glen Kim in Knox County Circuit Court on behalf of Jamie McClay as personal representative of the Estate of Johna McClay, deceased. The suit contained a single count – wrongful death. It sought an unspecified amount of compensatory damages -- in excess of $50,000 for jurisdictional purposes. This meant that the sky was the limit on how much the jury could award. Punitive damages are not allowed in wrongful death cases in Illinois or Matthew would have asked for those as well.

Matthew beat the two-year statute of limitations by one day. He had made no prelitigation demand on Glen, and he did not intend to settle the case. He wanted a jury verdict against Glen in an amount which would financially devastate him and his family, just as Glen had devastated the McClay family. Matthew pled the case in a way which alleged only intentional rather than negligent conduct, thereby foreclosing the possibility that Glen's liability insurance carrier would defend him. Matthew did not want insurance proceeds, and he didn't want Glen's defense of the case to be funded by an insurance company. He simply wanted to destroy Glen personally. Kyle was paying with his incarceration. Glen had to be held to account as well, and if the Knox County State's Attorney's Office wasn't going to take any action against Glen, then he would. This is how Matthew would deal with his grief.

Glen was opening the market that brisk November morning when he was approached at the door by the process server, a Knox County Sheriff's Deputy, who dispassionately presented Glen with the Complaint and Summons and stated simply: "You are served." Glen read the caption of the suit, "In the Circuit Court of the Ninth Judicial Circuit, Knox County, State of Illinois – Jamie McClay as the Personal Representative of the Estate of Johna McClay, deceased vs. Glen Kim". He felt his face flush, his pulse quicken and his ears start ringing. He was unable to read another word, and he didn't need to. He instantly knew that he was in for the fight of his life. Despite what everyone said to him, Glen already felt horribly guilty about having accidentally killed Johna. He had not had a decent sleep in the two years that followed. He relived the horror during Kyle Bastian's criminal trial and in his regularly occurring nightmares. His friends and family constantly reassured him that his actions had been entirely reasonable and justified and that the outcome had been a terrible accident the sole responsibility for which lay with Kyle Bastian. He had a hard time accepting this, but now his sense of guilt would have to give way to his instinct to fight. He became angry. Angry like he had felt upon learning that Scott had been shot to death. He didn't deserve this.

Glen arranged for his employee, Josh Hernandez, to staff the market that day and went home, where he laid on the couch on the back porch with the suit papers on this chest. He went over a million scenarios in his mind. He couldn't imagine telling Lin about the suit. As strong as she was, this would be a gut punch for her. But he would. And together they would do what was necessary to mount a defense and beat this case. Glen and Lin had not been able to save a great deal of money. They were by no means wealthy people. They lived hand-to-mouth, having spent most of their savings to meet their contributions to their daughter's education expenses and weddings. They might have to take out a second mortgage on their home and the market, Glen thought.

Matthew came home from the office that night and Jamie, who knew what he had been up to that day, was waiting for him. She had verified the Complaint signed by Matthew.

"Matthew, are you sure we are doing the right thing?" Jamie asked.

"Can you let me get my coat off at least, Jamie?" asked Matthew.

"I just don't feel comfortable suing that poor man, Matthew. I think he's as much a victim as Johna is." said Jamie.

"Oh yeah? Well, that victim gets to go home to his wife every night!" Matthew bellowed.

"Do not scream at me you asshole!" Jamie gave back.

"You know what, Jamie, maybe you ought to get off your goddamn fat ass and get to work instead of sitting home, drinking your wine and worrying about shitheels like Glen Kim!" yelled Matthew.

It was on.

"Are you going there you fucking bastard? Are you really going there?" Jamie yelled.

"Why is it that I'm the only one who gets up every morning and goes to work and does something about this situation?" asked Matthew.

"What do you mean by 'this situation'? You mean Johna's death? Is that what you mean? Well let me tell you something, Matthew. Suing the hell out of Glen Kim and ruining his family and store will do absolutely nothing to bring Johna back! You know that, right?" said Jamie.

"You don't tell me how to grieve or to do my job, Jamie! I will handle my business." Matthew responded.

Matthew stormed into the master bedroom and slammed the huge wooden door. It reverberated throughout the massive house.

"Don't you slam the fucking doors in my house!

Don't you slam that door on me!" Jamie screamed, as she opened another bottle of merlot.

Carter McClay was upstairs and heard the fight. He cringed at the vitriolic exchange between his parents. It was extremely uncommon for his parents to fight like that, but it seemed to be happening more often since Johna died. It was very painful and frightening to hear.

As expected, the Kims' insurer declined to provide a defense to the McClay lawsuit because the allegations involved solely intentional conduct on Glen's part. No negligence was alleged. Their policy excluded coverage for intentional acts, which was standard for policies of that nature. Their insurance agent even wrote a letter to the company imploring it to change its position, but to no avail. Their insurer would neither defend them nor indemnify them for any judgment that might be entered against Glen. They had nowhere to turn. Glen had no parents from whom to borrow funds. Lin's parents were quite elderly and impecunious. They would rather die than ask their daughters for money, and Glen and Lin formed a pact to lie to their daughters about the cost of defending the suit. Neither did they think a "GoFundMe page" was realistic. They were stuck funding the defense of this expensive suit on their own. Glen even suggested to Lin that she should divorce him in an effort to save at least some of their assets – a proposal that was immediately and vociferously declined. A second mortgage it would have to be, after liquidating Glen's gun collection along with every other asset they had that wasn't absolutely necessary for their existence. And when that money was gone, they would be at the end of their rope, but together.

The Kims' family attorney, Jeralyn Lark, explained that bankruptcy was not an option because the act alleged was an intentional tort, and therefore any judgment obtained would not be subject to discharge in bankruptcy.

"The Bankruptcy Code does not let you get relief from a judgment entered against you in a civil case for an intentional tort, and this Complaint alleges only an intentional tort." explained Jeralyn.

"So, what you're saying is even if we file for bankruptcy protection, we can't avoid this lawsuit?" probed Glen.

"Well, that's right. We could slow the process down a bit, but the McClays would be allowed by the Bankruptcy Court to lift the automatic stay and pursue this case. There is just no way out of this predicament but to win." Jeralyn stated.

"And if we don't win. If I get a judgment entered against me, how does it get paid if I don't have any money to pay it? Why don't I just allow them to take a judgment against me?" asked Glen.

"Well, I certainly don't recommend that approach, Glen. The judgment creditor – the McClays – would execute on their judgment by having your assets liquidated with the proceeds paid to them, and they would garnish your bank accounts and your income. Of course, they would liquidate the capital stock of Schrodinger's Market, Inc., too." said Jeralyn.

"So, they would get my store, my house, my savings and my income?" asked Glen.

"Well, that's complicated. You have a modest homeowner's exemption under Illinois law, and Lin owns half the house. Also, I advised you to place ownership of the house into a tenancy by the entirety. So, the McClays would not be able to execute on your home until Lin was deceased, and then they would have to pay you approximately $15,000 out of the proceeds of the sale of your house. I assume you own your home mortgage free, correct?" Jeralyn continued.

"The house and store are paid off." said Glen.

"And you have some small exemptions applicable to personal property. For example, you could keep your clothing, family photos and a bible. You would also be able to keep your equity in one vehicle under $2,400 and then equity up to $4,000 in any other property." Said Jerlyn.

"Oh my God, Jeralyn. How can that be? Even my old truck is worth more than $2,400 so I guess they would sell that too. I don't even have a bible. How is a person supposed to live under those circumstances?" asked Glen.

"You simply have to win this lawsuit, Glen.

That's the bottom line here." Said Jeralyn.

This was the type of debt that would result in their complete financial dismantlement. The McClays would be entitled to satisfy a judgment by executing on almost all of their property, except for certain exemptions which in the State of Illinois were anything but generous. The sense of financial anxiety was overwhelming, and both Glen and Lin were as nervous as they were angry at this prospect.

"What are we going to do, Lin?" Glen asked.

"We're going to win, Glen. It's just that simple. We have to put our trust in our lawyers. We will cross each bridge as we come to it." Lin replied.

Glen and Lin met with the defense lawyer recommended by Jeralyn. Amos Robinson resembled an aging Lieutenant Columbo, the character played by actor Peter Falk in the crime drama series of the same name. All the way down to the tan trench coat and self-deprecating manner. Amos was not to be underestimated. He was in his seventies and nearing retirement from the practice, having tried jury cases for the better part of half a century in west-central Illinois. But he had more than a few good years left, he thought, as he considered the challenging assignment. The retainer of $40,000 didn't do anything to dissuade him either. He was on board.

Amos was a partner in the largest and most respected law firm in the area. His office was located in Galesburg on the second floor of the bank building at the corner of Cherry and Main. While the bank had gone through several owners over the years, the law firm of Barnes, Sterns & Robinson had been a tenant for several generations. The other name partners had predeceased Amos, leaving him the most senior member of the firm of ten attorneys. Amos's office was stately and tastefully decorated. The walls in his office were filled with accolades and souvenirs of past victories. His ego wall behind his desk included his diplomas from Oberlin College and the University of Illinois College of Law, and a certificate from the Supreme Court of Illinois attesting to his licensure. Photographs of his wife, daughters and dogs took up most of the space on the credenza behind his desk and surrounded the laptop computer which looked good but in Amos's practice was more of a paperweight. His desk itself, an impressive replica of The Resolute Desk in the oval office of the Whitehouse, was immaculate. Not a single object, book, file or piece of paper was to be found on the surface. He had a large black leather couch in the back of the office and three black leather client chairs facing his desk. Glen and Lin found them very comfortable and listened intently to what Amos had to say.

Amos knew Matthew McClay well. The two had butted heads in the courtroom many times, always in a civil and professional manner, of course. Amos gave the Kims an honest and well-founded assessment of the strengths and weaknesses of Attorney McClay, the greatest flaw being the fact that he was clearly emotionally invested in the representation. But Matthew was a solid lawyer. He had a well-rounded general practice and handled a number of personal injury cases.

Amos then turned to the merits of the case itself. Amos had spent some time reading the Complaint and considering Glen's position. He had reviewed the Illinois Wrongful Death Act and had pulled up a few recent cases involving decisions in cases of this nature. Amos had also followed the Kyle Bastian case in the media, and Glen gave him a copy of the videotape that had been featured in Kyle's criminal trial. In all likelihood, Amos predicted, the case would survive motions to dismiss or for summary judgment and would make it to a jury of twelve Knox County residents who weren't clever enough to avoid serving jury duty. The case had been assigned to Judge Wilma Henderson, a fair but relatively timid jurist who preferred to allow weak cases to go to a jury rather than throwing them out for legal insufficiency. It was harder to get reversed by the appellate courts if you sent the case to a jury, and Judge Henderson didn't like to get reversed.

"Judge Henderson is one of the best judges in the circuit ... when she's sober." Joked Amos in his peculiar sense of humor. Amos recalled a continuing legal education seminar he had attended where Judge Henderson had been a member of a panel of judges answering "view from the bench" questions. Judge Henderson had shared that she liked to sustain one party's evidentiary objections after sustaining several of the other party's objections, so that things appeared fair. Amos was not a fan. He never forgot this comment, as it was an uncommon and frightening glimpse into the true thinking of a sitting trial judge. He decided not to share this story with Glen.

"This has all the attributes of a land war in Asia." explained Amos. "It's going to be a long slog, at best. And the outcome is anything but certain. But I will commit to you that I will give this my all, and if you will follow my advice throughout, I believe we can beat this."

Glen was comfortable with Amos, or at least as comfortable as he was ever going to be, and he signed the retainer agreement and tendered the large cashier's check. Amos then asked Lin to allow Glen to meet with him alone to discuss certain aspects of the case that would remain confidential and subject to the attorney-client privilege. Lin moved to the firm's conference room, and Glen shared with Amos his full, unabridged account of what had happened that night two years ago. From a legal perspective, the bottom line was that Glen had intentionally discharged his shotgun intending to kill someone. While he had accidentally shot the wrong person, the question would be whether Glen had acted reasonably under the circumstances having been in fear for his own life or the life of another thereby justifying his use of deadly force. A jury of his peers would have to put themselves into his shoes and determine whether Glen had met that standard. All Matthew McClay had to do was prove his case by a preponderance of the evidence – more probably true than not. Glen had the burden on his affirmative defense.

This case would be fought on the issue of liability and not about the value, or lack thereof, of Johna McClay's life – a somewhat risky strategy, but calculated to avoid angering the jury with arguments and evidence focusing on the value of the decedent's life. Under Illinois law, a successful plaintiff in a wrongful death case will be entitled to recover damages for the full pecuniary loss suffered by the next-of-kin as the result of the death. Amos's trial experience had taught him that issues of this type were a minefield for a defense attorney. That would be especially true with a decedent as young and distinguished as Johna McClay had been. Sometimes it was better to focus your artillery on the question of whether your client was legally responsible or not, and to ignore altogether the question of damages. If you won, you won big. If you lost, you lost big.

Glen and Amos discussed the pros and cons of impleading Kyle Bastian as a third-party defendant in the case. In the end, they made the same decision Matthew McClay had made, to leave Kyle on the sidelines. There was nothing really to be gained by obtaining a judgment against a judgment-proof slug like Kyle, and his inclusion in the litigation might only serve to complicate things.

"You can't squeeze blood out of a turnip, Glen."

Remarked Amos.

Amos had already started to develop the theme of the case. It was simple, obvious and elegant. Kyle Bastian, the empty seat in the courtroom, was the one who caused Johna's death. Glen had only been reacting to Kyle's deadly threat and conducted himself as any ordinary reasonable person would have under those circumstances.

Amos had also explained to Glen that he had a right to ask that a different judge be assigned to his case. Amos recommended against it, and Glen followed that advice. The bench was not very good in Knox County. It was better to stick with Judge Henderson than take a chance of drawing someone even worse.

Finally, Amos suggested that Glen might consider allowing him to file a motion to disqualify Matthew as the attorney for Plaintiff in the case. There was a decent chance that the trial judge might agree that Matthew's position as one of Johna's next of kin created a conflict of interest which precluded him from representing Plaintiff. By the same token, if Matthew were disqualified, Plaintiff may end up with a better lawyer who wasn't so emotionally involved in the case. If such a motion was to be filed, it needed to be filed at the outset of the case. Glen agreed that it was best to allow Matthew to continue to handle the plaintiff's case.

As Glen and Lin left the office, Amos summoned his secretary, and one of his paralegals into the conference room overlooking Main Street. Amos's secretary was Carolyn Hamilton, who had been with Amos for years and was Amos' absolute favorite co-worker. The paralegal, Kelly Greene, was relatively new to the firm. She was an interesting and colorful character who was so smart and good at what she did that she was encouraging Amos to delegate more than he had in the past. Outside of work, Kelly was a true bohemian, but Amos wasn't concerned about her private lifestyle, even though it wasn't in keeping with the staid and conservative image of his law firm.

"Let's put an Appearance and an Answer on file immediately. There is no sense in wasting time and money on a motion to dismiss. The Complaint is simple and well pleaded, and there is no way that Judge Henderson will dismiss the case. We're not going to play games with the pleadings. I want to serve Matthew with a set of written discovery requests along with the Answer and I want our private investigator, Jay Ashworth, to give me a full work up on Johna McClay. We need to know everything there is to know about her." explained Amos. "Finally, please order a complete transcript of the Kyle Bastian trial."

The next day, the Answer was filed generally denying the operative factual allegations of the Complaint and setting forth the affirmative defense that Glen had acted in self-defense. The Answer's prayer clause asked that the case be dismissed with prejudice. The Answer was short, concise and, in true Robinson style, got right to the point in plain language.

Amos's cellphone didn't stop ringing. One reporter after another called to get him to comment on the case. Amos was "old school" when it came to the media. He had earned his stripes at a time when lawyers didn't give press conferences designed to influence potential jurors and inflame the passions of the community. Not only did Amos believe that was unethical, he thought it was bad for his client.

"I encourage you to read our pleadings filed in the case, and beyond that we have no intent to try this case in the media. We will have no comment." Amos responded to each of them. Amos then called Glen and supplemented his advice to him by instructing him to avoid making any comments to the media about his case. Amos had already advised Glen to be tight lipped about the facts of the case and his confidential discussions with him, but Amos thought it wise to double down on that advice as it related to inquiries from the media.

"I know we talked about this generally, Glen, but I want to make sure that you don't make any comment to any reporters about this case, right?" advised Amos.

"Absolutely. I understand. I will keep my mouth shut." Glen agreed.

"These things tend to get out of control in the media, Glen, and you may feel an overwhelming sense that you need to have your story told. Resist that urge.

It always backfires." said Amos.

"I hear you. I will let you do all the talking, Amos." said Glen.

Matthew McClay followed suit, and the news media were left to thumb through the carefully crafted legalese of the court filings to find something to report. But there was no shortage of opinions from people on the street. Some sympathized with Glen. Some sided with the McClays. And disturbingly some saw a racial angle in the case and speculated how race would affect the outcome. The community seemed to pick sides early and easily and would prove to be almost evenly divided. Social media was abuzz. Too small for a Black Lives Matter chapter, Galesburg nevertheless did have an NAACP branch, and members from that group got involved and began a campaign on social media platforms in support of the McClays.

Not unsurprisingly, in the community, the case became primarily about race. In these times of social unrest, everything is about race. Somehow in the Kyle Rittenhouse case in the neighboring State of Wisconsin, in which a white 17-year-old shot three white rioters, the media and politicians saw the case through a racial lens. It was about white supremacy and structural racism they said. So, too, with McClay v. Kim. A Korean shop owner shoots an unarmed black woman in the back in his store. Stylized photos of Johna McClay started showing up at lightly attended protests, with the caption "Say Her Name." Small bands of protesters fanned out around the square carrying signs that encouraged passers by to "Honk for Johna!" and "No Justice No Peace". Schrodinger's Market was picketed on a semi-regular basis, with two or three people standing on the sidewalk outside brandishing homemade signs suggesting that Glen was a racist murderer. One sign said "She died. You can't hide." The college students, staff and faculty of Knox College organized a march from Old Main to downtown Galesburg near Schrodinger's Market to protest structural racism in the American justice system. None of this had anything to do with the facts and law applicable to the McClay case.

To be fair, the McClays did nothing to fan the flames. They neither encouraged nor discouraged this viewpoint. At Matthew's direction, the case was going to be tried in a court of law and not the court of public opinion. In fact, Jamie McClay began to dissuade Matthew from continuing with the suit, as she saw it potentially causing irreparable damage to the community and their standing in it. Jamie was concerned for the community as a whole but more particularly for how her remaining children would be received. She had never been much for the idea of filing the suit, and she had expressed her opinion to Matthew on several occasions. But ultimately Matthew's steadfast, single focus had won out. He would not, on the other hand, abandon his professional ethics and principles as he saw them, and he viewed the gathering political and social storm with disdain.

That didn't stop local politicians, however. After first gauging which way the political winds were blowing, several left-leaning office holders weighed in that this case would be a test of whether the American civil justice system was able to provide equal treatment under the law to Black litigants.

"Black people get the short end of the stick in the courts. The courts were just created as a way to return Black slaves to their masters. They are part of the systemically racist system." Pontificated Penelope Richardson, the Democrat Chair of the Knox County Board.

Others, on the right, suggested that this case had broader implications for gun rights for all Americans.

"This is nothing but a direct attack on our Second Amendment right to keep and bear arms in this country." professed a local representative of the Illinois State Rifle Association. And that mirrored the talk in all the local gun stores.

It seemed as though everybody had an agenda and was attempting to superimpose that agenda on this simple, tragic case, which had nothing to do with race, slavery or gun rights.

CHAPTER 14

Discovery

Discovery is the phase of litigation where each side attempts to find out what the other side is hiding. Its like a high stakes game of "Go Fish." Each side asks questions that the other side is required to answer truthfully. It usually begins with a flurry of written questions and requests (called interrogatories and document production requests). It also involves investigation of the facts of the case through subpoenas to third parties. Paralegal, Kelly Greene, was primarily responsible for promulgating the written discovery requests for Plaintiff and putting together Defendant's responses to Plaintiff's requests. Kelly pulled out the discovery requests the firm had used in the last wrongful death case they defended and used it as a form to start.

In the McClay case, there were a number of witnesses that both parties wanted to depose or question under oath, including Kyle Bastian, Officer Kolby Franklin and the medical examiner who had performed the autopsy on Johna. Glen gave his deposition, as did the entire McClay family and an economist they had hired. Discovery in the case took many months during which period the Court would hold quarterly case management conferences attended by the attorneys and a judge for purposes of making sure the case didn't languish. There was no risk of that with the McClay case. Both sides worked this case up promptly and thoroughly, all without judicial intervention. But with each such hearing in the case, the media would issue a new report on the case and further incite the ill will surrounding the matter. Cars were now bearing bumper stickers saying, "Justice for Johna".

One aspect of discovery involves the trading of witness lists. Each side discloses to the other who they plan to call as witnesses at the trial. Plaintiff disclosed, among others, an expert on the use of deadly force, a female police officer from Chicago named Jill Brandon who provided firearms training and instruction on the side. According to Plaintiff, Officer Brandon would testify that Defendant had used excessive force under the circumstances and had fired indiscriminately in Johna's direction proximately causing Johna's death. Of course, Defendant also disclosed an expert who was slated to contradict that conclusion.

Most noteworthy on the witness list for Defendant, however, was a person identified as a Marine Investigations Officer from Washington, D.C., who was going to testify about Johna's aborted court-martial for torturing a Taliban prisoner to death. Kelly had included this witness at Amos' direction. This piece of information had been uncovered by Jay Ashworth, the private investigator Amos's firm had hired for this case.

Jay was a mountain of a man. He was probably six feet two inches tall and weighed at least 400 pounds. He carried that weight well. He was intimidating to say the least. Covered with primarily self-administered tattoos, he wore shorts and short sleeved shirts all year around. He had served several tours in Afghanistan as an Air Force helicopter door gunner for a search and rescue unit. His military experience allowed him to understand how to get to the right people to investigate Johna's military record. He had found the information related to the Marine Corps investigation of Johna. It had actually made him feel even more respectful of Johna, as he too had wanted to kill Taliban non-combatants for the horrible way they treated women and children. Dogged though he was in his work, Jay had been unable to uncover any other pertinent information concerning Johna.

What possible relevance might that evidence have in this civil trial? Well, it went not to the issue of liability; but rather, it was pertinent to the question of damages -- the value of Johna's life. Had Johna lived and been successfully prosecuted by the government for such a serious violation of the Uniform Code of Military Justice, she would likely have been incarcerated for a lengthy period, thereby interfering with her earnings and the relationships she would otherwise have had with her family. This, in turn, would have reduced the pecuniary loss suffered by the McClay family. While Amos had made the strategic decision not to put on this type of defense at trial, from a tactical standpoint Amos wanted Matthew to fully understand how excruciating and grotesque this type of litigation could be. Frankly, Amos suspected that the undue prejudicial affect of this evidence would be found by the Judge to substantially outweigh its probative value and that it would, therefore, likely be inadmissible. There was no way Judge Henderson would have allowed Amos to conduct a trial within a trial on this issue. Nevertheless, Amos wanted to put a shot across Matthew's bow. This was not going to be pretty, and if the McClays wanted to move forward with their case, there were no holds barred.

On the other hand, Plaintiff's witness list had a surprise for Defendant as well. Matthew's investigation of Glen had disclosed a sale bill for a public auction of many of the Kim household assets, including Glen's full collection of guns and ammunition. The auctioneer was identified on Plaintiff's witness list as prepared to testify to the extent of Glen's collection and how unusual it was. Of marginal at best relevance, it was doubtful this evidence would be admitted at trial. However, Plaintiff did not wish to be outdone by Defendant in this vein. Plaintiff wanted Defendant to know how cruel things could get.

Witness lists were not generally filed with the court. Instead, they were turned over from one party to the other along with the filing of a Notice of Service of Discovery Documents informing the court what type of document had been served. However, there were many ways for information of this type to ultimately make it into the public domain.

At the close of discovery, Amos prepared and filed a motion for summary judgment stating that there were no genuine disputes as to any material facts in the case and that, assuming the truth of those facts, the law did not support a case to be presented to the jury. Kelly had performed some of the important legal research for the brief submitted with the motion. She had found some good case law supporting the motion that appeared to be "on all fours" with the facts of the McClay case.

"I found a great case, Amos. It's from the Third District Court of Appeals, and it involves a wrongful death case arising out of a self-defense shooting." reported Kelly.

"Fantastic, Kelly. What was the procedural posture of the case on appeal?" asked Amos, as he reached for Kelly's printed copy of the case.

"It was an appeal by Plaintiff from the grant of a motion for summary judgment by the Defendant." she replied. "It has some great language regarding the law applicable to self-defense."

"That's helpful. Good work. Thank you. I'll take a look. See if you can find a case that discusses the jury instructions for self-defense. You might start with the manual of pattern jury instructions for civil cases, especially a wrongful death case. See if there are any cases cited there. If the court denies our motion, we are going to need case law on that point." said Amos.

Amos's motion was asking that Judge Henderson dismiss the case, submitting that all of the relevant evidence pointed to Kyle Bastian as the person legally responsible for Johna's death. Matthew filed an eloquent response, brief and statement of facts as well, and boldly made the request that Plaintiff be awarded judgment on the issue of liability as a matter of law. After reviewing the evidence submitted by the parties and considering their arguments and authorities, the judge felt it best to have the jury decide this case.

Amos was not surprised, and neither was Glen in light of Amos's prediction at their first meeting.

"Well, that was a colossal waste." complained Kelly.

"Not at all, Kelly." explained Amos. "This was an opportunity to start educating the judge about our theme of this case. That was time very well spent, and your work was invaluable."

Matthew was thrilled. He wanted a full jury trial.

In preparation for a jury trial, the parties typically file motions seeking to limit the evidence that can be used by their opponent. These are called motions in limine. These motions state what they believe the other side is going to attempt to introduce and seek a pretrial order from the court precluding or limiting that evidence. One common motion in limine involves insurance coverage. The fact that the defendant in a civil suit is insured is inadmissible. As important, if not more so, the parties will ordinarily attempt to exclude evidence they believe will have an undue influence on the jurors such that they will be prejudiced against them and render a verdict based not on the relevant facts but on some incendiary piece of information.

Of course, both sides in the McClay case filed motions to bar the other from introducing the specious evidence disclosed in their witness lists – Plaintiff as to the court martial and Defendant as to the gun collection. Kelly prepared a draft of Defendant's motion in limine, and Amos finalized it. Matthew prepared Plaintiff's, as he was not utilizing the firm's support staff and resources to pursue his suit. As soon as the motions hit the court file, the media started calling again.

The media had a field day with this information which was now disclosed to the public in the court file. Glen the gun nut was trying to blame the victim and trash Johna's reputation. At least that was the narrative the local media ran with. Glen felt completely deflated. He did not understand how he had become so unpopular with the media and apparently the community who was consuming that media.

Amos called Glen.

"You might want to ignore the local media for the next few days, Glen." Amos stated.

"Well, it's too late for that, Amos. I heard on the radio this afternoon that my strategy was to smear the good name of Johna McClay and drag her memory through the mud." Glen said.

"As you know, that's not true. The jury will never hear a disparaging word from us about Johna. That you can count on. Just as we discussed." said Amos.

"I understand. The media is just out of control on this case. It's hard to bear." said Glen.

"I know, Glen. All I can offer is that I want you to hang in there. Have faith. And don't talk to the media." said Amos.

"I won't. Believe me." said Glen.

Moreover, Judge Henderson deferred her ruling on both motions in limine until trial when she would have a better understanding of the proposed evidence and how it may or may not be relevant. "Never decide anything you don't absolutely have to decide right now" was Judge Henderson's motto according to Amos. Everything seemed to be angling toward a full-fledged "shoot out at the OK corral" at trial. While Amos didn't relish that notion – he preferred a more orderly, predicable trial – he was quite used to it. That was the hallmark he used to say of any litigator worth their salt. You needed to show up, have a plan, but adapt and overcome. "Avoid the ambush" he used to counsel his younger partners and associates cutting their teeth on trial work. "Your plan won't survive first contact with the enemy," Amos taught. Have a theme for your case, and have an elevator speech about it, but be nimble enough to make adjustments on the fly. You didn't want to get caught flat footed.

Amos had doubled down on his theme of the case: Kyle Bastian, the empty seat in the courtroom, was the one who caused Johna's death. Glen had only been reacting to Kyle's deadly threat and conducted himself as any ordinary reasonable person would have under those circumstances. The true agent of this tragedy was not present. The key was now the jury instructions.

This case would turn on what instructions the judge gave to the jury regarding the law. Jury instructions can be very complicated, and it is a wonder that jurors seem to be able to understand them at all. Amos usually blew up the key instructions on poster board and used them at trial as demonstrative exhibits during his closing argument. He didn't want to look too sophisticated or "slick" for fear the jury might think he was being paid for by a deep pocket insurance company. But he allowed himself this single indulgence when it came to the instructions. Amos had been working on the jury instructions for the case since the day he took the case. The first thing he had done was crack the Illinois Pattern Jury Instruction book for civil cases and review the important instructions as it related to wrongful death and self-defense. He had built his defense around those instructions.

Settlement of the case was not in the cards as far as Matthew McClay was concerned, and he made that fact very clear to Amos and Judge Henderson. Matthew wanted to have his day in court. Despite this, Amos had at several points throughout the case obtained settlement authority from his client and made offers to Matthew consistent with that authority. Amos did not have a lot of money left to appropriate for settlement, but the Kim sisters had called a family meeting with their husbands and parents and insisted that a settlement fund be put together for Glen. Together, the family had been able to find and commit the sum of $250,000.00 to settle the McClay case. It was $250,000 more than the case was worth. But the peace of mind and risk avoidance it offered was priceless.

"You raised us, paid for us to go to college, and helped us pay for our weddings, Mom." Park said to Lin. "We are going to help you with this ridiculous lawsuit."

"You girls don't need to get caught up in this mess, Park." Lin said. "We can handle it, and I'm convinced we will win."

Yun joined Park in insisting that they be allowed to help. The girls had hired their own attorney in Chicago, a friend Park had gone to school with at Northwestern. She had reviewed the pleadings in the case and had suggested to the girls that an appropriate settlement range had $250,000 as its upper bound.

"Together, we are giving Dad a quarter of a million dollars to get this case resolved. That's the price of peace in this matter." said Park.

John and Ian chimed in, "All four of us have discussed this and we all agree, Dad. Life has been very fortunate for us financially, and we can certainly afford to help in this way. We insist that you let us help you end this nightmare."

"This is so generous, kids. You know I can never repay this. I will be forever indebted to you." said Glen as he wiped the tears from his eyes.

"Nope. That's what family is for, Dad." said Yun. "No strings attached."

The sum was deposited into an interest-bearing account in Lin's name alone at the Farmers & Merchants Bank in Galesburg. The gift tax consequences would be addressed by the kids.

With Glen's consent, Amos offered Matthew $150,000.00 with an eye toward increasing the offer as trial approached. When that was summarily rejected by Matthew, Amos suggested nonbinding mediation. That, too, was rejected out of hand. Matthew would not even give Amos the courtesy of a counteroffer, no matter how lofty or ridiculous. Immediately before trial was scheduled on the jury trial calendar, Judge Henderson asked the parties how far apart they were on settlement discussions. The Judge simply wanted to get a better feel for whether this case would settle and therefore come off the calendar which would allow another case to be scheduled in its place. Matthew told the judge what he had explained to Amos. "I can't put a number on the value of my daughter's life. I will leave that task up to a jury." said Matthew.

This case and the community were headed for trial.

CHAPTER 15

Voir Dire

The prospective jurors shuffled into the Knox County Courthouse and down to its basement, where they sat. And they sat. The Courthouse at 200 S. Cherry Street in Galesburg was a four-story, stone building with a dank basement resembling a dungeon. The building had been constructed between 1884 and 1886, after the county seat was moved from Knoxville to Galesburg. It was not a luxurious piece of architecture. If one of the jurors had forgotten to bring a book with them, the time passed slowly and without their cell phone (which were not allowed in the Courthouse) it seemed like an eternity. Then six at a time they began to be brought upstairs for jury selection, or voir dire.

"This sucks!" said one of the prospective jurors to the group.

"Are you telling me the County can't afford better accommodations for its jurors?" asked another.

"I don't know. This is better than being at work." suggested a third.

"Your job must suck, dude!" replied the first.

The tenor of the discussion was not elevated beyond that, and the prospective jurors who had elected to keep their thoughts to themselves each wondered how the justice system can actually function when our public education system was clearly failing. Do you really get a jury of your "peers" in this county, they wondered?

Picking a jury of twelve would prove a fairly difficult task. Many prospective jurors on the panel were dismissed for cause on motion of one of the parties. That is, many residents of Knox County had already formed a hardened opinion about the correct outcome of the case due to their exposure to the fairly intense media coverage, community demonstrations and marches, bumper stickers and social media posts. Others were close friends with the parties or had a particularly ingrained dislike for one of the attorneys. But one by one, the jury box filled up, and after two days and with all peremptory challenges having been used, voir dire was over. The case was ready for opening statements the following morning.

The twelve members of the jury with two alternates looked like Knox County. The parties had studied intently the answers each had given to the jury questionnaire. Neither the plaintiff nor the defendant had utilized the services of a jury consultant. Neither could afford it, and both lawyers had scads of experience picking juries and knew what they were looking for. Four of the fourteen were Black. Three were Hispanic and the rest were White. Six were male and eight were female. Most were older, with three who were clearly senior citizens. None appeared to be very young. They were farmers, retirees, mechanics, nurses, and stay-at-home mothers. Most had high school diplomas. Some didn't. Two were college graduates. Both sides felt this was a jury they could work with.

Amos and Matthew went back to their offices and worked on perfecting their opening statements late into the evening but then went home and to bed to get a good night sleep before what was expected to be a long week of trial.

CHAPTER 16

The Trial

With all assembled in the courtroom, and housekeeping matters out of the way, Judge Henderson instructed the bailiff to bring the jurors into the courtroom and the jury box. All stood as the jurors entered and took their seats. The courtroom, the largest and most grand in the Knox County Courthouse, was ugly. It couldn't hold a candle to any federal courtroom or to many of the other county courtrooms throughout the State. Several marginally successful efforts had been made to modernize and remodel it over the years. The County Sheriff, the County Board and the Administrative Judge all participated in that process, and it was obvious. It is said that a camel is a horse designed by committee. Well, this courtroom was fairly utilitarian and usable, but it did not inspire a great sense that anything important was transpiring inside. It was nevertheless packed. Several members of the media were present, along with a large number of interested citizens and nosey Courthouse staff. Kelly Greene was also present.

The Judge swore in the jury and read to the jury a brief summary of the issues in the case, prepared and agreed to by both Plaintiff and Defendant. The Judge then asked both parties if they were ready to proceed. Both indicated that they were. Plaintiff's counsel, Matthew McClay went first. He stood from counsel table, left Jamie sitting there by herself and approached the lectern from which he would deliver his opening remarks. After an awkward pause, he began.

"Ladies and gentlemen of the jury, as you know from voir dire my name is Matthew McClay, and I represent the plaintiff in this case.

Almost three years ago, on the eve of Thanksgiving, the lives of the McClay family were shattered and altered forever. The evidence will show that on that evening at approximately 6 p.m. an attempted armed robbery took place at Schrodinger's Market on Main Street in downtown Galesburg while twenty-six-year-old Johna McClay was present inside. The store's surveillance video recorded the actions of the three people in the store at that time: Kyle Bastian, who intended to rob the store; Glen Kim the defendant in this case, who owned the store; and Johna. We will show you the videotape along with the testimony of Kyle Bastian, Defendant, the medical examiner, an expert on use of force and Galesburg Police Officer Kolby Franklin. That evidence will show that Defendant, Glen Kim, intentionally pointed a loaded shotgun at Johna and deliberately pulled the trigger killing her instantly as Johna had heroically attempted to restrain Kyle Bastian. Bastian discharged his handgun injuring Defendant. All but Johna survived.

The evidence will further show that Johna died leaving two brothers a mother and a father, each of whom had a warm, loving relationship with Johna. You will hear from them how their lives have been devastated by the loss of their sister and daughter. We will present the testimony of an economist concerning the financial blow suffered by the loss of Johna.

At the conclusion of the evidence, we will ask that you return a verdict finding Defendant at fault for Johna's death and awarding Plaintiff damages in an amount aimed at trying to make Johna's family whole for their loss."

His uninspiring opening statement concluded, Matthew returned to counsel table and his wife and sat beside her not looking at her or the jury. Glen met Amos's gaze and raised his eyebrows. Maybe allowing Matthew to remain as Plaintiff's counsel had been the best strategy after all. Despite his bizarre refusal to discuss settlement, he was not delivering the type of impassioned representation he was known for. Perhaps he was holding back for fear of breaking down in front of the jury. It was hard to tell, but that, Glen and Amos agreed, was a lackluster opening.

Judge Henderson asked Amos if he was prepared to give his opening statement, and Amos rose smartly and approached the lectern.

"May it please the court and counsel. Good morning ladies and gentlemen. I am Amos Robinson of Galesburg."

It was crucial that the jury understood Amos was not some fancy, out-of-town shark coming into their territory to interfere with justice in the Knox County tradition. Amos always made sure he explained that he was from Galesburg when he tried a Knox County case.

"I am proud to represent Glen Kim, a Galesburg resident, who for decades has owned and operated Schrodinger's Market downtown. Glen's wife and daughters were shocked and horrified to learn that their father and husband had been gravely injured by Kyle Bastian as Kyle attempted to rob Mr. Kim with a handgun pointed at him."

Amos made sure to call Glen by name rather than refer to him as "Defendant" or even "my client". He wanted to humanize him and let the jury know that they were dealing with a human being here. Amos then slowly and carefully laid out for the jury the important facts of the case, explaining which witness would testify to which facts, and informed the jury about the key videotape. Finally, Amos made the jury a simple promise.

"As the defendant in this case, Mr. Kim does not bear the burden of proof on Plaintiff's claim, as the judge will later instruct you. Nevertheless, we will prove the elements of Mr. Kim's affirmative defense of self-defense. In that vein, we will demonstrate five things in this case, and I want you to hold us to that promise.

First, we will prove by a preponderance of the evidence that Mr. Kim discharged his lawful firearm at Kyle Bastian in an effort to eliminate the deadly threat that he reasonably believed Bastian posed to Mr. Kim and Mr. Kim's friend and customer, Johna McClay.

Second, we will prove by a preponderance of the evidence that Mr. Kim was correct to perceive Bastian as a deadly threat and discharged his firearm at the same time that Bastian fired at him, with Mr. Kim being struck in the chest by a .45 caliber bullet from Bastian's gun.

Third, we will prove that, simultaneously, Johna McClay lunged in Kyle Bastian's direction in an apparent effort to subdue him, and the shotgun blast intended for Bastian tragically found Johna instead, leading to her tragic and untimely death.

Fourth, we believe the evidence will show that at all times Mr. Kim acted lawfully and reasonably in self-defense to protect himself and Ms. McClay.

Finally, we are convinced the evidence will make it clear the person truly responsible for Ms. McClay's death, Kyle Bastian, is not present in this case or this courtroom.

We will ask that you carefully consider the facts of the case as presented by the evidence and that you carefully consider the law as given to you by the judge and, finally, that you return the only verdict appropriate – a verdict for Defendant, Glen Kim."

Amos sat down. At counsel table, Glen was very pleased. From behind the bar, Kelly thought it was masterful.

For the next four days, the jury was shown the evidence, including the videotape from the store that night, the testimony of numerous witnesses, and the certified conviction record of Kyle Bastian. Judge Henderson granted both parties' motions in limine, so the jury did not hear about Glen's gun collection or Johna's legal troubles. Plaintiff's economist testified that the discounted present value of Johna's projected future income was well over $2,000,000. Jamie testified that Johna had been a very industrious and thrifty young woman who had showed much generosity toward her family. Jamie, Clyde and Carter all testified to the grief, sorrow and mental suffering they experienced and their close relationships with Johna. Amos declined to cross-examine them. The evidence came in mostly without objection, and certain facts had been stipulated to by the parties. At bottom, the pertinent facts were not disputed. The question was what the legal impact was of those facts.

At the close of Plaintiff's rebuttal case, the judge and attorneys went into chambers where they conferred regarding the jury instructions. And this was the most critical phase of the trial. Both parties understood that the case would turn on the substance of the self-defense instructions adopted by the judge and given to the jury. Each party submitted their proposed instruction and the caselaw supporting their position. Amos argued for a standard, pattern instruction. Matthew argued for a modified instruction that included the concept that a defendant was not privileged to use deadly force against someone who was not posing a threat, and that a defendant had a duty to exercise ordinary care in exercising self-defense not to harm others.

Amos prevailed, and the judge would give the following instruction:

"A person is justified in the use of force when and to the extent that he reasonably believes that such conduct is necessary to defend himself against the imminent use of unlawful force. However, a person is justified in the use of force which is intended or likely to cause death or great bodily harm only if he reasonably believes that such force is necessary to prevent imminent death or great bodily harm to himself."

After the jury had received most of the court's instructions, the parties gave their closing arguments, with Plaintiff proceeding first and last. Matthew focused his argument almost exclusively on the issue of damages. He recounted the heart-rending testimony of his wife and two sons. He reiterated the findings and conclusions of the economist who testified about the discounted present value of Johna's projected future earnings had she survived. He argued that no amount of money would make the McClay family whole, as Johna could not be brought back to them. Finally, he told the jury that he trusted them to place an appropriate award of damages together given those factors, and he asked for a judgment in favor of Plaintiff.

As with his opening statement, Amos would be concise and cut to the chase. He began with the following instruction:

"If you decide for the defendant, Mr. Kim, on the question of liability, you will have no occasion to consider the question of damages."

He had blown it up and printed it on a poster board. He did the same with the instruction regarding self-defense. He placed those poster boards directly to his right and left as he addressed the jury. Knowing he would draw an objection, Amos first stated: "Glen Kim does not have insurance coverage for this."

Matthew immediately objected and stood with a look of astonishment. Amos asked the Judge if counsel could approach the bench. A brief sidebar was held outside of earshot of the jury.

"While the presence of insurance coverage is not admissible, there is no law suggesting that the lack of coverage is inadmissible." stated the judge. "That said, Mr. Robinson, I would have preferred this be submitted to me in advance of argument. You are experienced enough to know that. No more surprises."

"I understand, your Honor. I apologize." responded Amos, knowing that he had narrowly escaped. It is sometimes easier to get forgiveness than it is to get permission, he thought. In any event, the jury now knew that any award against Glen would have to be paid by him alone and not some wealthy insurance company somewhere.

The sidebar ended with Judge Henderson overruling Matthew's objection.

Amos resumed his argument:

"This case must be decided on the question of liability. Mr. Kim is not liable. Mr. Kim was clearly justified in the use of force because he quite reasonably believed that shooting at Kyle Bastian was necessary. It was necessary to defend himself against the imminent use of unlawful force by Kyle Bastian. In fact, Mr. Kim was justified in the use of force which was intended or likely to cause death or great bodily harm. He was justified because he reasonably believed that shooting Kyle Bastian was necessary to prevent imminent death or great bodily harm to himself. When you have someone pointing a gun at you and ultimately shooting you, all within a matter of a few feet away, and you are lawfully armed with a weapon yourself, it would be patently unreasonable and frankly suicidal not to fire your weapon at your attacker. The fact that the shot Mr. Kim took, with a split second to aim, was errant and accidentally took the life of Johna McClay is not a factor for you to consider. That was clearly not Mr. Kim's intention. It was clearly a tragic accident. Kyle Bastian is to blame for that, and Plaintiff for reasons only God will know decided not to sue

Kyle Bastian. That is the end of the inquiry.

Plaintiff has not alleged Mr. Kim was negligent or even reckless. Rather, Plaintiff has alleged that Mr. Kim intentionally shot Johna. We have fulfilled our promise to you in our opening statement. We proved for you the five facts we said we would. Accordingly, you have no occasion to consider the question of damages.

On Mr. Kim's behalf, I implore that you return a verdict in his favor finding him not liable for Johna's death."

It was noon, and after a few more instructions from Judge Henderson, the case would now go to the jury. The occupants of the courtroom stood once again as the jury was escorted to the jury deliberation room by the bailiff. With the expectation that it would likely take the jury a considerable period of time to reach a verdict, the courtroom emptied out, and the attorneys returned to their respective offices with the clerk to call them once the jury came back. The trial had been long and emotional. It was now in the hands of the jurors. What occurred in the jury room would be unknown. Just the verdict. How it was arrived at was off limits. It had been almost three years since the crime. It had been almost one year since the civil suit was filed. The competing senses of anxiety and exhaustion were real. Glen just wanted to go home and sleep, but he and Lin agreed to accompany Amos to the law office three blocks away to await the verdict.

Before they could walk that short distance down Cherry Street from the Courthouse to the law office, Amos's cell phone rang. It was the clerk, and the jury had informed the judge it had a verdict. This was bizarre, but very encouraging, as conventional wisdom is that the quicker the jury returns the more likely it is they have come to a defense verdict. Amos, Glen and Lin quickly turned and made their way back to the Courthouse. Glen had the feeling that he was floating the entire way. It was as though his feet were not touching the sidewalk. He was so anxious.

Glen had lost weight over the past nine months. His face looked gaunt, and his suit looked to be a size too big for him as he sat at counsel table with Amos. Glen prepared himself for both eventualities as he had so many times before during the pendency of this case. Matthew and Jamie looked spent as well. Both of them looked lifeless in their impeccable suit and dress, like they were merely going through the motions. Glen allowed himself for just a moment to imagine that maybe the McClays just wanted this case to be over as well, but he knew better. The courtroom was almost empty. Most observers had left for lunch and had not yet returned to the Courthouse to await a verdict. Nevertheless, Kelly sat in the front row on the same side of the courtroom as counsel table for the defendant. Clyde, Carter and the extended McClay family sat on the other side of the courtroom, also front row. A couple of reporters were present, as were a number of Courthouse employees.

It took Matthew and Jamie a few minutes longer to make it back to the Courthouse, but they soon arrived and resumed their place at counsel table in front of the bar. All stood as the jury reentered the courtroom.

The jury foreperson handed the verdict forms to Judge Henderson who cursorily reviewed them and handed them back. She stated, "Madame Foreperson, please read your verdict."

"We the jury in the above captioned matter hereby find for the defendant." stated the foreperson.

Glen tuned out the remaining formalities like the polling of the jury. It was over, and Glen thought that he would be elated and joyful, but instead he found himself with a fleeting sense of relief but an overwhelming sense of foreboding. In his gut, Glen did not believe this was the end. Amos and Lin were on top of the world. They hugged Glen. Together and then individually. And then they hugged again. Amos had done his job. The case had gone essentially as Amos had predicted. This instilled an even greater sense of trust and confidence in Amos on the part of Glen and Lin. It had cost them a great deal financially and in other ways, but it looked like the case and this unfortunate chapter of Glen's life was finally over.

Just then Matthew brushed by Amos at counsel table and, within earshot of Glen and Lin, stated: "We'll see you in the Appellate Court."

CHAPTER 17

The Appeal

The Third District Appellate Court, with appellate jurisdiction over Knox County, sits in Ottawa, Illinois. If there was to be an appeal in the McClay case, it would be heard first there. Appeals are heard by panels of three Appellate Justices. Successful appeals are rare. The Appellate Court generally affirms, and that is especially true concerning appeals from a jury verdict. Additionally, the Appellate Court has the power to award a party sanctions on appeal if the court finds the appeal to be frivolous. Amos had been to the Appellate Court numerous times and knew all of the justices on that court. Matthew was mounting an uphill battle.

A week after the trial, Matthew had filed a motion for a new trial in the trial court and, after a brief hearing and arguments by counsel, Judge Henderson had entered an order denying it. She did not believe that the jury's verdict was against the manifest weight of the evidence, the applicable legal standard, and she would let the jury verdict stand. Matthew had then timely filed his notice of appeal seeking a reversal of that order by the Appellate Court.

The standard of review on an appeal of this type is extremely deferential to the trial court. The Appellate Court looks to whether the trial court clearly abused its discretion in applying the legal standard applicable to a motion for new trial – again, whether the verdict was against the manifest weight of the evidence. A jury verdict is said to be against the manifest weight of the evidence when the opposite conclusion is apparent or when the findings appear to be unreasonable, arbitrary or not based on any of the evidence. Conclusions that are palpably erroneous and wholly unwarranted or outcomes which are the product of passion and prejudice will also justify reversal of a jury verdict.

Amos knew, as did Matthew, that this was an unsurmountable barrier in this case. The trial had been fair. The jury had followed the evidence and the law. The instructions had been appropriate, and there were no terribly controversial evidentiary rulings, including the trial court's rulings on the motions in limine. This verdict was going to be affirmed by the Appellate Court. But an appeal meant that the Kims would need to come up with more money to feed the meter.

Illinois Supreme Court Rule 375(b) states:

"If, after consideration of an appeal or other action pursued in a reviewing court, it is determined that the appeal or other action itself is frivolous, or that an appeal or other action was not taken in good faith, for an improper purpose, such as to harass or to cause unnecessary delay or needless increase in the cost of litigation, or the manner of prosecuting or defending the appeal or other action is for such purpose, an appropriate sanction may be imposed upon any party or the attorney or attorneys of the party or parties. An appeal or other action will be deemed frivolous where it is not reasonably well grounded in fact and not warranted by existing law or a good-faith argument for the extension, modification, or reversal of existing law. An appeal or other action will be deemed to have been taken or prosecuted for an improper purpose where the primary purpose of the appeal or other action is to delay, harass, or cause needless expense.

Appropriate sanctions for violation of this section may include an order to pay to the other party or parties damages, the reasonable costs of the appeal or other action, and any other expenses necessarily incurred by the filing of the appeal or other action, including reasonable attorney fees."

Amos wrote Matthew a letter immediately after receiving his notice of appeal. Amos quoted Supreme Court Rule 375(b) in his letter and informed Matthew that his handling of the case in the trial court and refusal to consider settlement had been abusive and that this appeal was clearly abusive and sanctionable. Amos warned Matthew that he would be filing a motion for sanctions in the Appellate Court if Matthew did not dismiss the appeal before briefs were due. To pay Amos for his defense of the appeal, the Kims took $25,000.00 out of the settlement fund put together by Park, Yun and their husbands. Amos would seek an order from the Appellate Court forcing Matthew to reimburse Glen for the amount of fees they incurred. Appellate courts don't like to award sanctions, but this case was different. Now the tables were turned slightly, and Matthew had skin in the game. If he lost on appeal, not only would he be denied a new trial, but he might be punished to the tune of thousands of dollars.

It was time for reconsideration of his strategy to hurt Glen Kim. Jamie told Matthew in no uncertain terms that this case must end, now. Matthew's law partner had expressed concern about the amount of time he was spending pursuing this litigation without earning fees. And Matthew did not relish the idea of spending the hours necessary to pour over the trial record and perform the legal research necessary to draft a persuasive appellate brief.

Matthew wrote Amos back. He stated: "We will dismiss the appeal for $200,000.00." Amos conferred with Glen, and Glen conferred with Lin. And they both talked to the girls. They had Matthew on the ropes now, but they also had the money necessary to meet that demand and end this case once and for all. It was a tough decision.

With the consent and direction of his client, Amos wrote Matthew rejecting his demand. "Mr. Kim rejects your demand and is not disposed to put any money on the table in light of his durable victory in the trial court. I would also like to remind you of my earlier letter and warning regarding our intent to seek sanctions on appeal."

Two days later, Matthew withdrew the appeal unilaterally.

Amos returned to Glen the $25,000.00 appellate retainer, and the Kims took that along with some of the settlement fund and, at the direction of the girls, paid off the second mortgage on their home and the market. The case was finally over.

CHAPTER 18

Kyle Bastian in Prison

Kyle Bastian did not end up in the same prison facility as his half-brother Mark. Rather, he was placed in the Pontiac Correctional Center, a medium security prison in Pontiac, Illinois. As with Mark, Ardis had no communication with Kyle and did not visit him in prison. Given her dementia, it was likely that Ardis had simply forgotten about Kyle. She declined rapidly after Kyle was gone. It was not that he had helped her out much. He had actually been a very self-absorbed son. But he had spent time at home with Ardis, and that interaction was probably good for her condition. Now her only interaction with the outside world consisted of her daily telephone calls with her neighbor and friend, Mary Carlson. She always had CNN, of course. She would need to be placed in an inpatient long term care facility before long.

Kyle did not fare well in prison. He wasn't cut out for it. He was constantly receiving write ups from the guards, who universally despised him. He was an insolent young man who bucked authority and seemed to have nothing to lose. Neither was Kyle taking advantage of the opportunity afforded him to finish his education in prison. He was not interested in rehabilitation. He would do his time the hard way and that was that. He hoped that he would be released at some point and still be able to have something of a life. But that was not to be. Kyle was beaten to death by another inmate in a disagreement over a pack of cigarettes. No one cared.

CHAPTER 19

Kolby Franklin

Kolby Franklin was glad to hear Kyle had been killed in prison. He felt bad that he felt that way, but he did. It served him right, he thought. What a colossal piece of human garbage Kyle had been. Kolby had not been able to get the images of the Schrodinger's Market shooting out of his head. As a police officer with some tenure now, Kolby had seen his fair share of the cruel and the disgusting. But his two run-ins with Kyle Bastian had been some of the worst. He would never forget the sight of the truck driver who had bled out on the floor of the Shady Lane Saloon after being skewered by Kyle with a broken pool cue. Moreover, he would never forget the sight of Johna McClay laying on top of Kyle with the back of her head blown off and his friend Glen Kim slumped over his counter with a bullet hole in this chest. That bell couldn't be unrung.

Kolby's fascination with all things quantum mechanics had not subsided. He was auditing a physics class on the subject at Knox College, and he had also talked the Athletic Director there into letting him use the indoor track and weight-lifting facilities. Kolby liked to stay fit by running and weight training.

He was a disciplined young man. He wanted to look good, and he wanted to have the strength and endurance to perform his job well. Unfortunately, Kolby's job as a police officer was quite physically demanding. Whether it was a domestic dispute or a foot chase in an auto theft case, Kolby regularly found himself scrapping with suspects. It had only become worse over the past few years, as the relationship between the police and some groups in the community had deteriorated, and more and more people attempted to resist arrest.

He had kept track of developments with the McClay civil case and felt justice had been done. He was greatly disturbed by the community's reaction to the case and the polarization and divisiveness it engendered. It tended to make policing more difficult and the city less livable. Throughout the proceedings, Kolby had continued to stop in at Schrodinger's Market and to touch base with Glen, but on advice of counsel, Glen had not been very forthcoming about the status of the McClay case. Kolby had received his news about the case from Courthouse gossip and from the local media. Kolby had the perspective to appreciate that the coverage had been extremely skewed and off the mark. The racialization of the matter by the media and politicians was damaging. Minority communities within the city may have grown even less trusting of the police. This lack of trust would manifest itself in many ways, not the least of which was the reluctance of witnesses to come forward and cooperate with the State in criminal cases. This would lead to a reduced rate of clearance on significant crimes. The very communities that were being hit the hardest by crime in the city were already declining to assist in the identification and apprehension of the offenders. Additionally, once a suspect was identified, the likelihood that suspect would attempt to avoid arrest or actually physically resist arrest was directly correlated with the engrained notion that the justice system didn't treat minority defendants fairly.

Kolby was aware of the pertinent issues and statistics. There is a general consensus in our society that, due to either subconscious bias or malicious motives, Black suspects and defendants are treated less favorably by the criminal justice system than are Whites. Observers allege that Black suspects are shot by police at a higher rate than are White suspects. They allege that Black drivers are pulled over more often by police than are White drivers as the result of racial profiling. They also allege that Blacks are more aggressively prosecuted and sentenced than White defendants in criminal cases.

The media tends to be attracted to incidents of White officers shooting Black suspects, and there are any number of anecdotal stories of this form of bias. In fact, the Black Lives Matter movement/organization was formed largely in response to instances of Black suspects being killed by White police officers. The heinous murder of George Floyd by a White police officer in Minneapolis was a glaring example. Interestingly, some of the most high-profile instances were found to be justified. Take, for instance, the case of 18-year-old Black man, Michael Brown, who was shot to death by a White police officer in Ferguson, Missouri in 2014. The facts of the altercation were disputed by many witnesses, but the FBI investigation, and a state grand jury investigation, found no basis on which to indict the police officer. This case ignited unrest in Ferguson and across the country and garnered national interest. Likewise, the case of Breonna Taylor, a 26-year-old Black woman who was fatally shot in her Louisville, Kentucky apartment in 2020 by White police officers, led to protests across the country. A grand jury declined to indict the officers for Taylor's death.

It is also true that the population of inmates in federal and state prisons in this country appears skewed heavily toward Blacks.

The statistics bear some of this out and throw a wet blanket on other claims.

Kolby had learned that the Stanford Open Policing Project collected statistics and analyzed the rates at which police stop motorists in locations across the country, relative to the population in those areas. The data showed that officers generally stop black drivers at higher rates than white drivers. This broad pattern persisted even after controlling for the drivers' age and gender. This was not consistent with Kolby's experience. He had no interest in harassing drivers, Black, White or Hispanic. He had much better things to do with his time. Honestly, he seldom knew the race of the driver of a car he pulled over until he approached the window. Racial profiling was simply not a reality for him in his police work.

With regard to police shootings, an exhaustive study by the National Academy of Sciences of the United States found no evidence of anti-Black disparities across shootings, and White officers were not more likely to shoot minority civilians than non-White officers. Kolby had never had to shoot any suspect, let alone a Black one, and he did not know any of his fellow officers who had.

Concerning arrest and incarceration rates, the Sentencing Project's Report to the United Nations stated that African Americans are more likely than White Americans to be arrested; once arrested, they are more likely to be convicted; and once convicted, and they are more likely to experience lengthy prison sentences. African American adults are 5.9 times as likely to be incarcerated than Whites. As of 2001, one of every three Black boys born in that year could expect to go to prison in his lifetime, compared to one of every seventeen White boys.

The United States Justice Department is presently investigating numerous municipal police departments throughout the country for racial discrimination in the application of criminal justice. In 2021, the United States Secretary of State invited the United Nations to conduct an investigation into structural racism in the U.S. criminal justice system.

As part of the criminal justice system, Kolby did not feel as though he individually, or his fellow officers collectively, treated Blacks or Hispanics any differently than Whites. Neither was it his experience that Black or Hispanic defendants were treated any differently by the Knox County State's Attorney's Office than were White defendants. If there was any differential treatment in the system, thought Kolby, it was based on class and not race. A poor White was more likely than a Black doctor to get a rough ride from the system, and that was a function of class. Wealthier, better educated individuals could more readily navigate the system. They didn't lose their jobs as the result of a court appearance. They aren't viewed and treated as dregs of society. They generally have better access to resources to pay their fines and to post bond. And they can afford to hire better lawyers.

Having a high-caliber criminal defense attorney represent you in connection with a criminal charge is a much different experience than that of a poor person who has no choice but to be represented by the Public Defender's Office. There is a reason why wealthy people spend money to hire expensive private lawyers.

Kolby believed that culturally, on a per capita basis, there was also simply more crime committed by the underclass. They were more likely to drive while intoxicated. They were more likely to abuse their spouse. They were more likely to shoplift. Not that these common offenses were never committed by the middle class (Galesburg didn't have many upper-class citizens), of course they were. But statistically these crimes were committed more by members of what Kolby liked to call the underclass – poverty so complete that you cannot climb out of it generation after generation. When Kolby drove by the yard at Henry C. Hill Correctional Facility and saw mostly Black inmates, he honestly believed that Black people were simply responsible for more crime in Illinois.

Although he had not grown up in a very diverse town, Kolby did not consider himself to be racist by any stretch of the imagination. Knoxville, Illinois had a population of approximately 3000, and the portion of White residents was over 98 percent. By contrast, Galesburg was ten times as populous and had a While population of about 84 percent. He bristled at the "Defund the Police" movement that he saw going on nationally with many cities. He despised the lack of respect and outright hatred for police that had taken hold. Those anti-police attitudes trickled down to Galesburg, and he saw the reportage surrounding the McClay lawsuit as substantially contributing to the problem. Kolby loved his job but his morale was low. He found himself musing about how much better life might be if he had pursued his interest in mathematics and become an actuary or a math teacher.

Kolby dropped by Schrodinger's Market in uniform after the civil case had concluded. He wanted to let Glen know that he was thinking of him and that he thought the case had the correct outcome. He noticed a new "Black Lives Matter" sign in the front window, which he thought was interesting. He entered and struck up a brief conversation with Glen. Glen was pleasant but slightly guarded. Getting ready to leave, Kolby asked Glen if there was anything he could do for him, and Glen answered in the negative. But as Kolby opened the door, Glen called to him.

"Ya know, Kolby. There is one thing you could do for me. Anything you could do to reopen the cold case of Scott Morrissey's murder at my store would be greatly appreciated. I would really like you to find his killer." Glen said.

"I understand, Mr. Kim" replied Kolby. He did not want to try to explain to Glen that he was a patrol officer and not yet a detective. It was an odd request, but Kolby considered it a sincere one. He tucked Glen's request away in the recesses of his brain with the idea that if he ever did get promoted to detective, he would definitely do his best to grant Glen's request. He was a problem solver with the intellect and passion to help Glen out in this way. He got back into his patrol car and continued to cruise the streets of Galesburg.

CHAPTER 20

Lin and Glen Kim Move On

Lin Kim was painting again. She had lost interest during the period following the shooting. But perhaps inspired by Hunter Biden's recent dalliance with art, Lin picked up her brushes, readied her oil paints and medium and put a blank canvass on the easel. There was now some hope of her having some commercial success with her art. After all, Hunter Biden's paintings were flying out of the gallery at prices exceeding those for Picassos.

Honestly, Lin hated Hunter Biden and all that he stood for. She hated the President and his entire family who she considered to be a clan of grifters. The Bidens were like ticks, dug into their national host and sucking the lifeblood out of it. The idea that Joe Biden received the largest number of votes in history was anathema to Lin. She just couldn't accept it. Demographically and occupationally, Lin's politics were somewhat unusual. Her now elderly parents had been very conservative and had raised her that way. She had maintained those conservative values even while at U.C. Berkley and despite her mostly progressive friends in the art community. She just didn't talk politics, to anyone. She kept her political beliefs close to the vest, although her artwork often contained clues.

Lin's first painting since the shooting was a portrait from a picture of the Reverend Martin Luther King, Jr. Her style was less realism and more impressionism. The portrait was almost a mosaic of color that resulted in what seemed to be a perfect likeness of King, one of her heroes. King's example and teachings had ushered in a new relationship between the races in this country – a relationship that measured one another based upon the content of their character rather than the color of their skin. Lin saw the new obsession with race, brought about in large part by critical race theory and Marxism, as a destructive leap backwards in race relations. She longed for the days when she grew up and when the goal was to be colorblind, not color centric.

As a Korean American woman, Lin had experienced prejudice growing up in California. She did not pretend to know what it must be like to be Black in America today, but she did not believe much of the rhetoric about structural racism, just as she eschewed the notion that her rights and privileges as a woman were any less appreciable than those of men. She looked at prejudice as an individual action, not a collective one. A person discriminates, she thought, not an institution. She had raised two girls who had gone on to great success in her mind. Their gender had not held them back in any way. She, herself, had been a successful artist, teacher and manager. To Lin, monetary wealth was relatively unimportant. Once you were able to afford the basic necessities of life, the measure of success was not financial. It was a function of whether you were able to achieve your other goals and aspirations in life. By that measure, she and her daughters were wildly successful people. This country that had allowed for that success was a truly great country wholly unappreciated by the progressive movement. Ironically, race relations had actually never been better in Lin's mind until the Black Lives Matter movement set us back sixty years. That angered Lin, but she allowed her feelings to be woven into her paintings and choice of subject rather than in arguments on social media or over the dinner table.

Much to her surprise, Lin had not lost her adjunct instructor position at Knox College in light of the fallout surrounding the McClay lawsuit. Lin had worried about that quite a bit. She worried that the cancel culture, especially on college campuses (and liberal ones like Knox College), would find her guilty by association with her husband who had wrongfully been labeled a racist.

Neither had the board of directors at the Galesburg Civic Art Center, an extremely liberal group, found it necessary to replace Lin as director over the controversy. Lin had been given a "heads up" by one of the more conservative members of the board and terrific artist, Ralph Smith. He adored Lin and wanted to make sure she understood there were rumblings among other board members that the controversy was not good for the non-for-profit center. Ralph wanted to make sure she did everything possible to avoid being the nail that sticks up.

Her staying power was magnificent. Lin's tight-lipped approach to her politics was part of it. But you can't overestimate the power of her competence and sheer talent and ability in those positions. Either institution would have been cutting off its nose to spite its face by discharging her.

She had swallowed her pride to accept a gift from her children to assist with the attempt to settle the McClay lawsuit. But she had considerably less heartburn over selling assets and borrowing money from the bank against their real estate. The financial blow to the Kim family – approximately $50,000 – was trying, but Lin believed that she and Glen would be able to survive just fine. Neither planned on retiring, and both had an adequate income to meet their modest needs. Finally, the girls and their husbands had filled that hole for them and allowed them to get rid of their mortgage payments. Fortunately for Lin and Glen, their girls and sons-in-law had been able to achieve substantial wealth in a short period of time. Investment banking and commodities trading had been quite lucrative, and they had been frugal in true Kim style. All were going to be just fine.

Lin had kept a low profile during the controversy. She had canceled her Facebook and Twitter accounts, using Snapchat and text with her daughters and close friends. The concept of "friend" had evolved for Lin. She had been reminded of the importance of being a true and loyal friend even when petty differences or politics made you see things through a different lens.

On the other hand, Glen struggled. His anger had subsided. He now saw the world as very transactional. He had become much more cynical, not just about law enforcement, but with everything. His only reliable home base, he thought, was his business and his family. Everyone else could go to hell. Not a religious man, Glen saw morality as something derivative of the social compact. He thought of it as a human convention and not in divine terms. His life had been hard, yet he had been a good and dutiful man. Other than his relationship with his wife, small family and employee Josh Hernandez, Glen did not see that he had a lot going for him. He didn't have a lot to show for his hard work and good conduct. The social compact wasn't working out for him. Instead, he had been shot, his friends had been killed, he had been wrongfully accused of intentionally killing someone, and he had been wrongfully characterized as a racist. That's not good for business. And all he knew was how to run a small convenience store. So, he did what he had to do. He didn't have any firmly held beliefs anymore. He was neither conservative nor progressive. He focused on the pragmatic. He didn't give a shit about the Bidens. Everything became relative. He became a chameleon. He put up a "Black Lives Matter" sign in the front window of his store, not because he supported the movement or group, but because he felt he needed it for business, and it tended to reduce the incidence of graffiti and vandalism. Glen no longer had a penchant for firearms or for building a gun room in his basement. He no longer volunteered in the community by coaching baseball or otherwise. He was no longer active as a member of the Galesburg Noon Lion's Club. He was all about business and family now.

As Glen and Lin both arrived home from work, they met in the garage. Lin had been sitting in her car listening to the end of one of her favorite songs – volume turned way up. She was winding down after a full afternoon with Art students at Knox. Glen pulled in beside her and smiled in her direction. Lin smiled back and gave Glen a flirtatious wave. Her head was gently bobbing from forward to back to the rhythm of the song. Glen got out of his truck and walked around to Lin's driver's side window, and she rolled it down. The music was still blaring.

"What in God's green acre are you doing, woman?" Glen joked.

"Hey, its 'Blackhole Sun' by Soundgarden!" Lin retorted as the song came to an end and she turned the car stereo back down.

"How was your day, Honey?" asked Lin.

"Good. I guess." replied Glen. "We ran out of Marlboro reds, and you would have thought the world was coming to an end."

"Did you have a run on cigarettes or something." asked Lin as the two walked into the house from the garage.

"No. Nothing unusual. I just forget to reorder." explained Glen. "But holy shit did I piss off some customers."

"I thought Josh was doing the ordering these days, Glen?" Lin stated.

"He does with most merchandise, but I still take care of the liquor and cigarettes." Glen replied. "Thank God I didn't run out of Busch Light! I might not have made it home in one piece tonight." Glen laughed.

Lin was stooped over looking in the freezer drawer of the refrigerator. "What are we going to fix for dinner?" She asked. "Everything we have to make is frozen. Should I try to defrost something?"

"How 'bout you let me treat you to dinner out tonight?" Glen posited.

"I could go for that, Honey!" Lin responded quickly. "We need to go to the Art Center for Ralph Smith's show tonight for a short while anyway. We can go right after we eat."

"Ralph is the one who puts manipulated photographs on aluminum, right. That sounds fine to me." said Glen. "I know he's one of your favorite local artists."

"That's right, Glen. He's very talented and a

really good person as well." said Lin.

Let me change my clothes and we can go, Lin. Where would you like to eat?" said Glen. "And what should I wear?"

"Just put on a sweater and some khakis, Glen." counseled Lin. "I'm not dressing up."

Their favorite restaurant in Galesburg was Koreana, a real Korean Barbeque place on Main Street near the Art Center. The food was fantastic, and the service was better. Owned by one of their friends, Koreana was their "go to" place to eat when they dined out. Glen had always felt welcome there, even during the trial.

"Let's do something different and go to Koreana." joked Lin.

"I'm game. That sounds fantastic, Lin" replied Glen. The evenings' plans were set.

CHAPTER 21

Josh Hernandez

Glen's young protégé at Schrodinger's Market for years was Josh Hernandez. Josh had joined Glen very shortly after Glen lost Scott Morrissey. Josh was a Galesburg native. His great-grandparents had come to Galesburg with the railroad in the late nineteenth century. They had landed in the south end of Galesburg near the railroad tracks and First Street, where they had lived in what essentially amounted to a railroad box car. Josh's great-grandfather had labored for the railroad his entire life, not an easy or glamorous job but it provided a living. Three generations later, Josh had the same work ethic and drive. He was trustworthy, and he was loyal to a fault.

After graduating from Galesburg High School, Josh went to Southern Illinois University in Carbondale, Illinois. He had enrolled in the flight program with the idea that he would be a commercial pilot. Unfortunately, Josh was unable to afford his tuition the second semester, despite working two part-time jobs. His parents were financially unable to assist him, and his scholarships and financial aid were insufficient. He had been taught by his parents and grandparents not to borrow money, but to pay cash having saved the amount necessary for the purchase. Debt was slavery they said. Accordingly, Josh had sworn off of student loans. Instead, he returned to Galesburg and went from business to business looking for work. He would save money and finish his education, he thought. When he dropped by Schrodinger's Market, having seen the "help wanted" sign, Glen hired him on the spot. That was one of the best decisions Glen ever made. That and marrying Lin.

Josh had met a girl a little older than him in Carbondale the first semester at college. Her name was Sarah McDermott. Sarah was an admissions representative for SIU and loved her job. When Josh was forced to move home to reside with his parents again, Sarah opted to stay in Carbondale. Four and a half hours was a long drive for them to maintain the relationship, but Josh reliably made the trek every chance he got. Josh and Sarah were inseparable, despite the distance between them.

Josh was a particularly handsome young Hispanic man with a round, clean-shaven face. He had dark hair that he kept short, and he was always well-groomed. Josh had big brown eyes to go with his big friendly smile. At five feet eight inches tall, Josh was not a large man, but he was extremely physically fit and loved to be outdoors, hiking, camping, or his new hobby of riding horses with Sarah.

Sarah was a good match for Josh. She complemented him well. Sarah was relatively tall for a woman standing five feet seven inches, and she was as thin as a rail. She looked fantastic in the stylish business attire she wore to work, but she looked even better and more comfortable in the western style out-fits and cowboy boots she could be found in on the weekends. She had classically beautiful features, and she didn't wear, or for that matter need, any makeup. Her tousle of long, blonde hair was curly and very nat-ural. She often wore it in up, but it looked great in any configuration. She, too, loved the outdoors. Sarah had grown up with horses, and she kept a horse of her own named Frosty stabled at a barn just outside of Carbondale. Frosty was a large white, fourteen-year-old gelding that stood 16 hands. Sarah had graduated from SIU with a bachelor's degree in animal science. She had been a competitive barrel racer in junior rodeo all through school and expected to have a career as a large animal veterinarian. However, Sarah didn't pursue veterinary school having instead accepted a position with the University as an admissions rep-resentative following her graduation. Her assigned territory was the State of Illinois, which didn't require much overnight travel for her, and she typically had her weekends free. Now, she liked to trail ride and did so often. Shawnee National Forest in Southern Illi-nois had a vast system of riding trails, and Sarah could regularly be found on those trails with Frosty.

Josh had never even touched a horse until he met Sarah. He was a city slicker. But Sarah changed that. The two of them spent most of their time together in the Forest riding or at the barn grooming and tending to Frosty. Sarah's friend Angela also boarded a horse at the same barn, and Angela was quick to allow Josh to ride her horse with Sarah and Frosty. Angela's horse was named Lightening, but his name belied his nature. He was a gentle, twenty-two-year-old, dead broke, sorrel gelding that knew the local trail system like second nature. Angela was happy that she had someone who was willing to ride him, because she travelled frequently with her work and didn't always have the opportunity to do so herself. Lightening was no pasture ornament and needed to be ridden.

Josh took to horseback riding like a fish to water. Sarah bought Josh a nice pair of goat skin Tecovas cowboy boots for his birthday, and she liked to dress him so that he looked the part. Josh and Sarah would take their bedrolls and gear with them and regularly camp overnight in the forest during the Spring, Summer and Fall. Sarah drove a big, blue Ford F-250 pickup truck with a gooseneck hitch in the bed and hauled a matching, four-horse trailer with a tackroom that easily housed her ample tack for two horses. She had room for a few bales of hay in a rack on top of the trailer.

Josh spent much of his time at the market daydreaming about hanging out with Sarah and the horses. He always earmarked a portion of his bi-weekly paycheck for his horse acquisition fund. When he was able to save $2,500, he would be in the market for a horse of his own that he would stable with Frosty in Southern Illinois. He was actually hoping that Angela might be willing to part with Lightening at some point now that she wasn't able to ride as much.

When he was at work, however, Josh truly enjoyed his job and was dedicated to Glen and the store.

As Josh and Sarah brushed the horses after a ride and put the tack away, Josh turned to Sarah and opened up about the market.

"I never liked the idea of Glen keeping a shotgun behind the counter." Josh said. "I don't feel comfortable around guns, and I knew that shotgun meant trouble."

"Did you ever talk to Glen about that?" Sarah asked.

"I did. I told him how I felt. He was just hellbent on keeping that gun there. He was so afraid of the same thing that happened to Scott happening again." Josh replied.

"I have to say I'm kinda with Glen on that issue, Josh." said Sarah as she walked Frosty to his stall.

"Why?" inquired Josh, turning his head to follow Sarah.

"We have a God-given right to defend ourselves, Josh. And I would rather be judged by 12 than carried by 6." Sarah said with emphasis as she closed the stall door after checking Frosty's water bucket.

"I just see how much trouble this caused for Glen though, Sarah. This trial has been absolute hell for Glen." said Josh.

"Right. I understand. But think of what might have happened had Glen not been able to shoot." said Sarah.

"Glen's shooting didn't resolve the threat. Johna hitting the robber in the head did. Glen's accidental shooting of Johna could have been avoided altogether if Glen had not been armed." said Josh.

"I see. That's true in that instance. But I just totally appreciate Glen's perspective on being armed and able to defend yourself." said Sarah. Sarah started to help Josh finish up with Lightening.

"You never put a horse away wet, Josh. Make sure you brush out the hair under the saddle, too." said Sarah.

"Okay. I will." replied Josh as he picked the brush back out of the tack box. Lightening stood in cross ties near the entrance to the beautiful horse barn – more of a carriage house, actually. It was a old wooden structure with gables and a shake shingle roof. The brass weathervane on the peak of the cupola could be seen for quite a distance reflecting the sun. The barn contained six large stalls, a tack room and feed room. It had large sliding doors at both ends and a man door on one side. Each stall had a window, and the natural light shone in to illuminate the straw dust hanging in the air. When both sliding doors were open the air moved swiftly through the barn minimizing the smell of ammonia and manure.

"That's 20-20 hindsight anyway, Josh. I hope you don't hold that against Glen." said Sarah.

"No. I get it. I don't. Glen is a phenomenal guy. It wasn't his fault. I just wonder how that gun truly contributed to the situation." said Josh.

Changing the subject, Sarah asked Josh where he wanted to eat. It was getting late in the afternoon, and if they went home to make dinner, they probably wouldn't eat until late.

Sensing they were going to have to agree to disagree on the subject of guns, Josh answered, "Let's order pizza on the way home. How does that sound?"

"Perfect. That sounds awesome. I'm so hungry" said Sarah as she topped off Lightening's water bucket and closed his stall door.

"Let's button things up and get out of here." said Josh. "Riding was a blast today."

Having started early in the morning, the two had covered ten miles of trails that day. The weather that Fall in Southern Illinois had been warm and dry. Josh and Sarah were taking full advantage of it. They decoupled the gooseneck trailer in the barn's parking lot and took off toward town.

CHAPTER 22

The Impact of the Trial on Matthew McClay

Matthew McClay's county seat law practice had not been negatively impacted at all by the past three years' disfunction. If anything, it seemed like the volume of his business was up. That didn't mean that the volume of revenue was up, however. His firm, McClay & Davis LLC, had seen better days. Matthew had started the firm as the Law Office of Matthew McClay LLC upon returning to Galesburg from Des Moines, Iowa where he had received his law degree from Drake University Law School. It had been difficult for Matthew to land a job with an existing firm, and he decided to hang his own shingle. Matthew attributed his difficulty in finding a job to the depressed economy, not to his race. And over the years, Matthew had made quite a name for himself in the legal community and among the residents of Galesburg.

The McClay trial had increased his visibility even more. Notoriety can be a positive thing these days. Name recognition, no matter what the association, seems to be the trick. Celebrity for the sake of celebrity is in vogue. Well, Matthew was notorious in Galesburg, and it drove a considerable amount of legal business to him and his firm. The problem was that west-central Illinois was a dying community. The money had dried up. Despite the burgeoning need for legal assistance, people in Galesburg couldn't afford much in the way of legal services on their social security income, their disability payments or their minimum wage earned income. Nobody had any savings and nobody's parents had any savings.

Matthew commiserated with his partner, Marsha Davis, about the financial predicament.

"Divorces are more common, but the parties lack the money to be adequately represented or to fully pursue their rights in court." Matthew complained to Marsha.

"Yeah, and defendants in criminal cases are typically poor enough to qualify for representation by the public defender's office." Marsha replied.

"People are going to Peoria for personal injury and employment law cases." Matthew lamented. "And there go our contingency fee cases where we might actually make some money."

"The damn insurance companies are then hiring Peoria lawyers to defend those personal injury and employment law cases here in Knox County." Marsha responded.

For the most part, those who were dying in the community did not have substantial estates, and the rules for charging fees in estate cases had changed significantly due to abuses from a prior generation of lawyers. The real estate transactional practice had become commoditized and substantially taken over by non-lawyer title companies. Income tax returns, even complex ones, were prepared by accountants or taxpayers using sophisticated software. Legal Zoom had cut into the business of incorporating small businesses.

"Bankruptcy clients are now using Peoria lawyers with laptops in the park for fees well below cost for a legitimate firm." Marsha added.

"True. It's like the cost-conscious consumers of legal services prefer to hire the

'bottom feeders' of the legal community who provide generally slow and incompetent services at unsustainable prices." Matthew stated. "Getting paid for legal services has become a real struggle."

But both Matthew and Marsha still managed to bring home a healthy draw and bonus.

Matthew's mix of cases included a smattering of almost everything. It was hard to stay abreast of changes in the law when he had to cover such a wide swath of specialties. He did, though. Attending a lot of continuing legal education classes, it was no problem for Matthew to meet his mandatory minimum number of hours every two years to maintain his licensure. He took his legal secretary and paralegal with him to most of those CLEs he attended as well, as Matthew leveraged them heavily in his practice to keep the cost lower for his clients. The main benefit of the breadth of his practice was that Matthew had something new and interesting to work on almost every day. This competency in many areas of law also made it easier for Matthew to take a *pro bono* case once in a while. He felt a duty to give back to the community in this fashion for the exceptional living it had provided to him and his family.

Marsha's practice very similar to Matthew's. Each had a similar clientele and new cases were assigned by the receptionist on an alternating basis unless a particular attorney was requested. Both had more work than they could handle. Marsha was a forty-five-year-old White woman from nearby Galva, Illinois. She had attended law school at the University of Illinois after graduating from Macalester College in St. Paul, Minnesota. She had responded to an add Matthew placed in the Illinois State Bar Association's Illinois Bar Journal for an associate, and Matthew knew a good thing when he saw it. The two got along famously, and Matthew made Marsha a partner after two years as an associate. She was smart and attractive, and she really had a way with people. She had hit the ground running upon her return to the area, as she and her family were well known and had a large network in Knox and nearby Henry Counties.

Matthew respected Marsha a great deal and relished his law partnership with her. He would cautiously avoid anything that might damage that relationship, and he had been greatly influenced by Marsha's stated concern about his pursuit of an appeal in the McClay case.

CHAPTER 23

The Impact of the Trial on Amos Robinson

Amos Robinson's practice was slightly different. He and his firm tended to specialize in certain distinct areas of the law and refer other types of cases to their partners and associates. To the extent an attorney kept a case that fell into another's expertise, they referred to that as hoarding. Hoarding was discouraged. The thought behind the scheme was that lawyers would only handle cases they were extremely experienced and skilled with, and that was the best way to deliver high value (high quality at reasonable cost) legal services to the client.

Amos used to joke that he specialized in "estate planning for the indigent", but in reality his specialty was civil trial work. He had cut his teeth and amassed a good degree of wealth earlier in his career when he would regularly be retained by large insurance companies to represent their insureds in defending auto collision cases and slip and fall cases in Knox and the surrounding counties. As that work dried up in small Illinois towns, Amos had transferred those litigation skills to private pay general civil litigation, including representing plaintiffs occasionally. Other lawyers in the area who handled transactional matters (estates, real estate, corporate and tax law) would regularly refer litigation matters to Amos because they could rely on him to competently handle the case for their client and to then return their client back to them. He earned his fees mostly by the hour at somewhere north of $400 per hour. In by 7:30 a.m. and usually not out until 6:30 p.m., Amos was a slave to the timeclock and the billable hour. If you stopped supplementing your retainer you got fired as a client - no exceptions. He didn't utilize technology as much as he could. His partners kidded him for being a Luddite. And Amos did not delegate much work to paralegals. He was comfortable doing things his way. He was a great mentor to younger attorneys in the firm interested in developing their trial skills and would often encourage them to "second chair" his trials with him.

Amos's practice had not been impacted by the negative publicity surrounding his representation of Glen Kim in the McClay case. Those clients utilizing his services tended to be fairly sophisticated and had looked at the outcome Amos had obtained in the case rather than the controversy swirling around his client. Frankly, Amos wouldn't have cared if it did negatively impact his practice. After all, he was close to retirement and as a matter of principle he believed that everyone, even the unpopular, needed to have good legal representation. He would regularly make that philosophy known at firm meetings where controversial representation was discussed. Most of the business attorneys and transactional attorneys preferred that the firm not take on any unpopular or controversial cases. It was thought that the firm's good clients – those in the community that still had a few cents to rub together – might go elsewhere rather than be associated with a firm that would represent a scoundrel. Amos almost preferred representing unpopular causes. He would also take on certain cases on a *pro bono* basis, but only intentionally and after careful consideration of the time investment it would take to complete the representation.

Most of Amos's contemporaries in the local legal community and some who were even younger had passed away or retired and moved away. They had not been replaced by young lawyers coming to town. Amos wanted to keep working, but he had seen a couple of his partners hang on a little too long. In fact, Amos had been the one who drew the short straw and had to confront his partner, Bill Sterns, about his waning competence and need for retirement to avoid malpractice claims -- one of the most singularly uncomfortable moments in Amos's career. Amos did not want to visit that type of burden on anybody else, and accordingly, he was prepared to retire at an age he considered to be still in the prime of his career.

CHAPTER 24

Galesburg in the Wake of the Trial

Naturally, as the McClay civil trial faded into history the controversy surrounding it did as well. It had left some scars, but the community moved on. There were new and different matters to be concerned with. Galesburg was not the type of city that would tolerate racism of any kind. It was an ethnically diverse city. Its history was one of abolition and equal rights. No single event of this nature was going to change its character. Galesburg was home to the first anti-slavery society in Illinois and had been an important stop on the Underground Railroad. The city's founders and early residents had shown remarkable resiliency, adaptability and progressive thought, especially when it came to the subject of race.

It was November, and the city square was already decorated for Christmas. In fact, all of downtown was dressed up for the holidays. Most of the storefront windows – the ones that were still in business – contained Christmas themed displays and some celebrated Chanukah with menorahs and stars of David. Kwanza and Diwali were not well-represented among the displays. The streetlights on Main

Street were decorated with wreaths, and the trees were strung with lights. The boutique stores and restaurants on Seminary Street looked very festive and bustling with business. The new condominiums above those businesses had their Christmas trees and candles in the windows, and it was nice to have people living downtown again. Galesburg's downtown looked clean and merry and alive.

Schrodinger's Market was an exception. Glen wasn't big on Christmas. He didn't put up decorations and Lin had long ago given up trying to persuade him to do so. It didn't affect business, according to Glen. The rest of Main Street, running East and West, outside of the downtown area, was mostly blighted. The houses needed paint. The commercial properties needed a facelift. The street and sidewalks were lined with weeds instead of trees. It was dominated by pawn shops, gas stations, dollar stores and fast-food restaurants, with a few remaining houses that had not yet been razed for commercial construction.

North of Main Street, the many large, two story Victorian homes on large lots laid out on a grid of beautiful, tree-lined, brick streets were decorated with Christmas lights. The fallen leaves had mostly been raked into brown paper lawn waste bags sitting at the curb. That said, Galesburg was "spotty" as Amos Robinson was fond of saying. It was not unusual to find an utterly rundown apartment house or two in the middle of a gorgeous stretch of well-kept neighborhood. The City of Galesburg did not do a good job of encouraging property owners to keep their properties looking nice or their lawns mowed, and the City was very reluctant to condemn houses that were dilapidated to the point of being dangerous eyesores. While those problems were fairly unusual in the north end of town, they were much less common in other small Illinois towns that were more aggressive on that front. Everything considered, however, the north end of Galesburg was a very pretty and comfortable place to live.

South of Main Street was a different story. What used to be lovely middle-class neighborhoods with large stately homes, small local markets and grade schools had devolved considerably. While some areas and neighborhoods had maintained their luster, a lot of them now looked dirty, old, disheveled and depressed. Nevertheless, the Christmas spirit was still alive and well in most of the south end. Decorations in those neighborhoods tended to include large blow-up Santas, snowmen and reindeer out on the front lawn in addition to strands of multi-colored lights on the roofline of the home.

Knox College was located in the south end of Galesburg. It had been founded in 1837 as a private, independent college, among the first institutions to admit women and people of color. It had been founded as Knox Manual Labor College by a Presbyterian minister, George Washington Gale, from upstate New York. Gale, along with a group of like-minded northeasterners, had set out west to establish a "thorough system of mental, moral and physical education" on the prairie in Illinois. While its first settlors arrived in 1836, the City of Galesburg was not incorporated until more than twenty years later. In 1930, Knox College absorbed Lombard College which had been founded by Universalists in 1851 in Galesburg. It, too, was located in the south end of Galesburg, and remnants of its campus are still present. Galesburg grew up around these two colleges. Knox College's small campus was very attractive and included very old as well as very modern architecture. As the neighborhoods around the campus deteriorated, Knox College bought up many properties to control the blight and to expand parking, athletic fields and residence halls.

Galesburg also had a two-year community college, Carl Sandburg College, established fifty years ago to serve Knox County and nine other surrounding counties. With about 2500 students, the yearly average tuition for the college was approximately $5,000 and over 63 percent of its students received grants and/or scholarships to attend. It was located on the northwest side of town. By contrast, the tuition at Knox College for its 1,100 students was over $50,000 per year, with fees, room and board being another $11,000.

Over the years, there was somewhat of a political rift between the north end and the south end, as those in the south felt that an unfair portion of the city's attention and tax money went to improve the north end. However, that rift had for the most part subsided.

Much of the new commercial construction, including big box stores, bank branches, chain restaurants and retail stores was occurring on the very north end of Galesburg. The south end was dominated by the railroad yard and what was left of the manufacturing and industrial economy. Galesburg still maintained two hospitals, and for a town of 30,000 inhabitants, that was unusual. One of the hospitals was a not-for-profit corporation owned by the Sisters of the Third Order of St. Francis, which gave it considerable staying power in the community. The other was owned by a for-profit company and struggled mightily to stay afloat and maintain critical mass. Both were located north of Main Street.

Galesburg's High School was also located in the north end. Its enrollment was sixty-five percent White. That included 788 White students, 175 Hispanic students, 139 Black students, and 128 students who identified as being two or more races. Only one percent of the students were Asian. The junior high school was also located in the north end. The enrollment at Churchill Junior High was thirty-nine percent minority. Lombard Middle School was located in the south end and had a minority population of forty-eight percent, with the lion's share of those minority students being Black. Seventy-seven percent of the students at Lombard were economically disadvantaged. The dwindling number of grade schools were distributed throughout town.

One of the largest employers in Galesburg was the BNSF Railway. Galesburg has for some time been a railroad town. The Atchison, Topeka & Santa Fe (AT&SF) Railroad built through Galesburg in 1887 on its way to Chicago. Now, with seven main rail lines going in and out of Galesburg, it is a transportation center. Additionally, the Galesburg train station was used by eight Amtrak passenger trains.

Galesburg had a relatively high crime rate, with 1,387 crimes reported annually in 2019, 138 of which were violent crimes. The most dangerous neighborhoods were located south of Main Street. The number of gun crimes and violent crimes was on the rise.

CHAPTER 25

The Death of Glen Kim

Glen Kim's left lung had been severely damaged by the gunshot wound he suffered at the hand of Kyle Bastian. Perhaps it was related to this condition, but Glen had become subject to bouts of pneumonia in the years that followed, and in late December, the day after Christmas, he passed away in a hospital room at St. Mary Medical Center. He was surrounded by his wife, two daughters and both sons-in-law. Glen's physician, Dr. Mark Mesker, had done everything he could for him. Josh was minding the store.

Lin was stoic, where Park and Yun were inconsolable. Everyone stayed at the Kim home on North Cherry Street until after Glen's funeral three days later. Many mourners attended Glen's visitation. Kolby Franklin who had been promoted to detective recently, was there to pay his respects. As was Amos Robinson. Josh Hernandez had closed the store to attend, and Sarah had taken time off to travel to Galesburg for the service. It was clear that Glen's life had touched the community in a very meaningful way. From his volunteer activities and his involvement in the Lion's Club, to his daily presence in Schrodinger's

Market, Glen had met and had an impact on a lot of Galesburg residents. While he didn't have a large family or a large cohort of close friends, he had made a profound impact on the community over his many years. Apparently, the hatred and rejection Glen had felt at the way the community had reacted to the McClay suit had been more of a product of his imagination and insecurity.

Glen was cremated as he had directed, and his ashes were interred at Galesburg Memorial Park Cemetery, near where the remains of Scott Morrissey had been buried.

Glen's Last Will and Testament had been prepared by the Kims' family attorney, Jeralyn Lark. In a letter attached to his Will, Glen had asked for an old-fashioned reading of the Will, and all obliged. At the attorney's office, in the presence of Lin, Park and Yun, as well as Josh, the Will was read. It was simple. No complex trusts or tax gimmicks. It didn't need to be, as Glen had very little by way of property at his death. Jeralyn unfolded the Will and read it aloud. It stated in pertinent part:

"I, Glen R. Kim, residing in Galesburg, Knox County, Illinois, being of sound and disposing mind and memory do hereby make, publish and declare this instrument to be my Last Will and Testament, hereby revoking any and all prior Wills and Codicils.

I wish to express to my wife and best friend that I have loved and adored her for as long as I have known her, and I cannot tell her how much I have appreciated her counsel and comfort over the good times and bad. I am so proud to have been her husband.

To my daughters and sons-in-law, I wish to express that I am infinitely happy that all four of you have each other and that you have pursued and attained your important life goals. I wish you the happiness and love I have had with my wife. You are destined for success in your future endeavors, of that I am sure. It was an honor to have you call me dad.

To all, I wish to state that I was never a man of means, and I will have little to pass along at my death. Most of what I had to give I have given during my lifetime. Nevertheless, as you know, the most important things in life are not material wealth but peace of mind, meaningful work and a loving family. I have had it all.

I nominate my wife as the executrix of my estate to serve without bond.

I direct that all of my debts, funeral expenses, and costs and expenses of administration be paid by my executrix in her discretion from the income or principal of my estate as soon as practicable after my death.

I hereby give an interest in Schrodinger's Market, Inc., an Illinois business corporation, consisting of 49 of the 100 issued shares of capital stock, to my loyal employee, Josh Hernandez, for his years of dedicated service.

I hereby give, bequeath and devise all of the rest, residue and remainder of my property, both real and personal, that I own at the time of my death to my wife, Lin Kim, as her sole and absolute property if she survives me, and if not to my children in equal shares, share and share alike."

Lin would be in business with Josh. This came as no surprise to Lin. In fact, it pleased her greatly. Her Will would give Josh her 51 shares. Josh was humbled. No one had ever given him anything, and this was an extremely generous gift in so many ways. Lin hugged Josh and neither could hide their emotions. Josh was now even more tied to Galesburg.

"Glen considered you family, Josh." said Lin.

"I don't know what to say, honestly, Lin." Josh replied.

"Well, you're going to need to hire a deputy of your own, Josh. Someone you can trust as much as Glen trusted and relied upon you. We're going to need some help." said Lin.

"I appreciate this more than you know, Lin." Josh said.

"It is me who is the lucky one here, Josh. I'm happy to be in business with you, and Schrodinger's Market lives on." said Lin.

Chapter 26 The Memorial

Following the funeral and after the reading of Glen's Will, as Lin sat in her kitchen alone carefully opening and reading each of the hundreds of sympathy cards and memorials, she noticed one particular memorial that didn't have a name or address on the envelope. She picked it up and looked at it for a minute and then she opened it.

It contained a plain note stating, "I am terribly sorry for the way I treated your family following my daughter's death. Glen was a truly good man. I wrongfully focused my anguish on Glen, to whom I should have apologized directly during his lifetime. I am ashamed of the unimaginable pain I must have caused Glen, you and your family. I know this does nothing to undo my transgression, but please use this to honor Glen in the manner you see fit." It was signed, Matthew McClay. And it enclosed a check for $100,000 made payable to Lin Kim.

CHAPTER 26

Solving Scott Morrissey's Murder

The first call Lin made after receiving the check was to Amos Robinson. She wanted his private investigator, Jay Ashworth, to investigate and help solve the murder of Scott Morrissey. Glen had gone to his grave without a sense of closure on that traumatic episode in this life. That was the best way to "honor" Glen, thought Lin. She would use what portion of the $100,000 it took to fund that investigation.

Amos gave Lin Jay's number, and she called him immediately.

"Mr. Ashworth, this is Lin Kim. I'm Glen Kim's widow." Lin opened.

"Oh, I know who you are ma'am." Stated Jay. "And please just call me Jay. That's what everyone calls me. Your husband was a wonderful man. I am so very sorry for your loss. What can I help you with?"

"Well, a number of years ago, Glen had an employee at Schrodinger's Market whose name was Scott Morrissey. Scott was murdered by someone who robbed the store in 2008, and the Galesburg Police Department was unable to close the case. To my knowledge the investigation stalled some time ago and nothing is being done." explained Lin. "I would like to hire you to help reopen that investigation and solve Scott's murder. Is that something you're interested in doing, and if so, how much would you charge for your services?"

"Ma'am, I would love to help you, and my fees are based on the hourly rate of $150 per hour plus reasonable expenses. No retainer is necessary. You can just pay as we go." Jay explained.

"You're hired, and please stop calling me 'ma'am'. I'm Lin."

Jay called the Galesburg Police Department to speak with Detective Kolby Franklin.

"Detective, this is Jay Ashworth. If you remember me, I'm a private investigator in town, and I'm handling a matter for Lin Kim." said Jay.

Kolby's ears perked up immediately. He felt goosebumps on his arms.

"I see. Does it have anything to do with Scott Morrissey?" asked Kolby.

"Actually, that is exactly what this is about." answered Jay.

"How can I help? Would you like to meet and discuss this?" asked Kolby.

"Absolutely. I mean, yes. Let's get together. Maybe you could meet me at the law offices of Barnes,

Sterns & Robinson. We can use one of their conference rooms, and it would be great if you could bring the contents of the GPD file with you." Jay responded.

"Let me see what I can do. Would tomorrow morning at 9:00 a.m. work for you?" asked Kolby.

"It would. I will meet you in the lobby tomorrow morning." said Jay.

Ever since Kolby had been promoted to Detective, he had thought about Glen's single request of him. He wanted to reopen that cold case and work it. The objects described by quantum physics are neither particles nor waves, but a third category that shares some properties of both, such as frequency, wavelength but also subject to being counted. It is foreign to our customary way of thinking about things. It taught Kolby that it was important to expand the way he observed and thought about his situation. He knew he would figure this out.

Kolby also knew the first hurdle to solving the puzzle was getting approval. The department did not have unlimited resources, however, and Kolby feared that the Police Chief would not be inclined to give him such an assignment.

Kolby approached Chief Robert Folger that afternoon with the proposition.

"This isn't about some quantum mechanics bullshit, is it Franklin?" asked Chief Folger.

"No, Chief. I'm not here to bore you with my

theories." said Kolby.

"Thank God, Franklin. What do you need?" said Chief Folger.

"I would like to work a cold case – the murder of Scott Morrissey on June 15, 2008 here in Galesburg" said Kolby.

"Well, do you have enough time, given your other work, you think?" inquired Chief Folger.

"I do. I will make the time Chief." said Kolby.

"What's your particular interest in that case, Franklin?" asked Chief Folger.

Kolby explained to Chief Folger how he had been challenged by Glen Kim and that Lin Kim was now pursuing the matter following her husband's death.

"That Kim was a good man. I knew him. He sure got a bad rap a few years ago in that crazy case brought by Matthew McClay. I think McClay is an asshole. Yeah, I'm on board, Franklin." said Chief Folger.

Kolby was off to the races. He grabbed the file and made copies of its entire contents, which wasn't much more than the initial police report. He scanned everything into his laptop and finished his shift before going home for the night. He poured over the details of each document in the file looking for that one item that would allow him to get ahold on this case. Kolby fell asleep in his chair.

The next morning, Kolby was up bright and early, went to the college to run and work out. Kolby got some breakfast in before venturing downtown to meet with Jay. He was anxious for the meeting. Kolby arrived and met Jay in the waiting room of the law firm. They were escorted to a large conference room overlooking Main Street, where the two reacquainted and looked at the police report and the few other miscellaneous documents in the file.

The police report recounted what was found at the scene and what the initial investigation had included. On June 15, 2008, at 9:00 p.m., Officer Johnson had responded to Schrodinger's Market on Main Street in Galesburg after dispatch had received a 911 call from a store customer, Mary Meeker. Mary had gone into the store and found the clerk, Scott Morrissey, dead and slumped behind the counter. She had called the police.

Mary was still on the scene standing outside when Officer Johnson arrived, and after checking Scott, securing the scene and calling for EMS, Officer Johnson had interviewed Mary. Mary seemed rattled, and she disclosed that she was forty-eight years old and resided at 1087 N. Cedar Street in Galesburg. She stopped by Schrodinger's Market on her way home from work as a waitress at a downtown restaurant. She had parked her car in front of the store and had seen nothing of note before entering the store at approximately 8:55 p.m. She saw no one else in the store. She intended to buy a few items and did not immediately see the clerk, but as she approached the counter, she saw the clerk slumped over on the floor behind the counter with blood pooled on the floor around his head. She reported that she had smelled the faint odor of gunpower as she entered the market. She immediately ran outside and dialed 911 on her cell phone. Her contact information was in the report. A criminal background search on Mary showed nothing but a few minor traffic offenses. She would not be a suspect.

Detective Rodgers then arrived at the scene at 9:10 p.m. He called and interviewed Glen Kim, the owner, over the phone. He was at home and had been there with his wife since shortly after 6:00 p.m. that evening. He learned that Scott had been employed by Glen for approximately ten years. He was slated to work from 6:00 p.m. to close at 10:00 p.m. There were no other employees in the store. Glen told Detective Rodgers that he did not have security cameras installed yet in the store. The register drawer on the counter was open and there was no cash except change in it. Glen estimated that there had probably been about $500 in the drawer based on store policy and average revenues.

Detective Rodgers had checked to see if there was any video footage of the store from any of the local businesses in the area, and none was found. No further evidence was found at the scene other than Scott's body and the bullet that killed him.

Scott's autopsy showed that he had been killed

by a single gunshot wound to the head. The bullet had exited and was found by Detective Rodgers embedded in the wall behind the counter in the center of a large pattern of blood spatter. The bullet was significantly deformed, but the forensics team from the Illinois State Police had determined that it was 5.7x28 millimeters (or .224 inches) in diameter.

That was going to be it, thought Kolby. That was an extremely uncommon caliber used exclusively in one firearm: The FN Five-Seven, manufactured by FN Herstal in Belgium. Kolby was familiar with this semi-automatic handgun introduced in 1998 but only to the military and police. It was then made available on the civilian market in 2004. It is used by the U.S. Secret Service and is a relatively controversial firearm, as the 5.7x28 bullet is capable of piercing body armor. Studies by NATO found that the 5.7x 28 cartridge was far more efficient than the much more common 9x19 parabellum (9mm). The rarity of this bullet was going to be key to the solution to the case, but it wasn't nearly enough. They needed something more.

After an exhaustive search, no shell casings had been found at the scene, and it was assumed that the killer had taken the time to retrieve the shell casing before leaving the scene. As such, there was no opportunity to examine the shell casing for fingerprints. No further evidence or witnesses were identified, and at this point, there was absolutely nothing to take to the State's Attorney.

Jay and Kolby decided that the only way to

restart the investigation was to reinterview Mary Meeker, if she could be found ten years after the crime. However, the effort to reinterview Mary Meeker was stalled when they discovered that she no longer lived on Cedar Street and had left no forwarding address with the Post Office. The phone number she had given to Detective Rodgers was not in service. The neighbors did not know where Mary had gone. A skip trace did not show a current address.

They needed someone to come forward with information. Why would anybody do that, especially ten years after the fact, when the incident had faded from the minds of most? Money. That's what might make somebody come forward – cold hard cash. They needed to offer a reward for information. And they needed to use social media to get news of the reward out.

The discussion with Lin went very well. After sharing the status of their investigation, Jay and Kolby broached the subject of a reward.

"Lin, we both believe that adding a monetary reward to a Facebook post would be much more inclined to produce results. It's a real longshot in the first place, but without offering money to someone to come forward with information, I don't know that we will have any chance of success." explained Kolby.

"How much money are we talking about, guys?" asked Lin.

"Well, there is no science to it, but I would recommend somewhere in the neighborhood of $5,000 to $10,000." said Jay.

"Done. Let's offer $10,000. If we need to, we can go up from there." said Lin, now smiling at Kolby and Jay.

The Facebook post was made that afternoon with the offer of a $10,000 reward. Both Kolby and Jay felt like kids on Christmas Eve, waiting to see what was under the tree the next morning.

Pauline LoBianco checked her phone as she got out of her car in front of her boyfriend's rundown apartment building where she had been living with him for a couple of months. It was located on busy N. Henderson Street. The two had been together for six years, but Pauline had just recently been talked into moving in with him. Her parents, siblings and friends had all counseled against the move, but Pauline had followed her heart.

She was returning home after tanning at a salon that morning. Her phone said it was 10:59 a.m. on Saturday. She checked her Facebook app and scrolled through the posts on her feed. As she walked to the apartment, she noticed a post from the Galesburg Police Department that had been shared by one of her Facebook friends. The post said "$10,000 reward for information leading to the arrest and successful prosecution of the person(s) who killed Scott Morrissey at Schrodinger's Market in downtown Galesburg, Illinois on June 15, 2008." Her blood ran cold.

Pauline stopped and paused for a moment before entering the apartment, No. 121. Her boyfriend, Brandon Anderson, was inside likely sleeping off a hangover from last night's partying. She instantly knew that this post related to the story Brandon had told her years ago after a night of drinking. He had confided in her that he had been the one who robbed Schrodinger's Market and shot the clerk years before. Pauline had not been sure Brandon was being honest with her. She thought he might just be bragging or trying to scare her and making things up out of whole cloth. However, she recalled news reports of that murder and had a friend who had known Scott Morrissey. They had talked about the murder at the time as it had hit so close to home for her friend. Pauline had often wondered about that confession and what Brandon was actually capable of. She knew he was a violent man who had a serious substance abuse problem, but he had never mentioned it again. She just couldn't bring herself to believe that Brandon had actually done what he told her he had. It was much easier to disbelieve his story. She loved him.

Pauline entered the apartment. Brandon was asleep on the couch in the living room, with the television on and tuned to an adult cartoon show. The apartment was dark with the shades drawn on the only window. She went into the bathroom and sat on the side of the old bathtub. She once again looked at the post. She decided that she was not going to believe that Brandon had been involved, and she wasn't going to say anything to anybody about it.

Brandon woke up and lumbered into the bathroom, his head in his hands. He unzipped his jeans and urinated as Pauline sat on the tub.

"You look like you're a hurtin' unit, dude." said Pauline.

"Oh my God, my head is splitting." Brandon responded. "I think I need a drink."

Brandon zipped his pants and reached for the Advil in the medicine cabinet above the sink.

"Yeah. That's a good idea." Pauline said sarcastically.

Brandon cupped a handful of tap water from the sink faucet and swallowed it with several of the Advil tablets. Pauline looked at him and wondered to herself whether this was the best she could do. She was thirty years old. She had a decent job. She was reasonably attractive, she thought. She was smart. She had friends. She had a good personality. Was Brandon Anderson the man she wanted to spend her life with?

"You smell like burnt skin, Pauline." Brandon scoffed as he turned and walked to the refrigerator.

"What a catch." She mouthed to herself.

Brandon Anderson was thirty-two years old. He was a libertine. He had graduated from nearby ROWVA High School in Oneida, Illinois. He grew up in the small town of Altona, Illinois and had moved to Galesburg after school to find a job. The going was tough early on, and Brandon had bounced around from one kitchen to another as a cook. He made very little income, and it had not been sufficient to support his drinking and use of methamphetamines. He had tried to supplement by dealing a little bit, but that didn't solve the problem. He had off and on relationships with several women, all of whom had eventually moved on. Brandon met Pauline when he was in the kitchen at The Park House restaurant in downtown Galesburg and she had just started as a waitress. Shortly after the two met, Brandon was discharged by the manager for absenteeism. Pauline stayed and still worked there as the waitstaff manager. Brandon applied for a job with the BNSF Railway but failed the drug test. He wasn't eligible for many jobs due to his extensive criminal record which included convictions for misdemeanors as well as felonies, including disorderly conduct, domestic assault, robbery, possession of methamphetamine with intent to deliver, violation of an order of protection and two DUIs. He had been the respondent in three order of protection cases brought by former girlfriends, one of whom was the mother of his daughter born out of wedlock after the two had split up. Brandon paid no child support, and the mother was more than happy to forego the support to keep Brandon away from her little girl.

Brandon's past substantially limited his employment options, as did his seeming inability to show up to work reliably. But Brandon appealed to Pauline because he was tall and good looking. He was thin but muscular, and when he wasn't blind drunk, he was usually fun and talkative with an engaging personality. He pulled the wool over the eyes of many. Presently, Brandon was working at one of the two KFC fast food restaurants in town making about $15 per hour forty hours a week. His income combined with that of Pauline allowed the two to barely scrape by, and most of their disposable income was spent at the bars.

That night, Brandon and Pauline went out to the bars. With friends, they tied one on. When they got home, the situation was volatile. Brandon was a mean drunk and jealous. That was not a good combination. The neighbors in apartment 122, were used to hearing Brandon and Pauline scream and fight in the early morning hours most weekends. Today was no different.

"You just couldn't stop yourself from flirting with Jason, could you? You couldn't stop." Brandon said to Pauline slurring his words as they walked in the door.

Jason was a friend of Pauline's who they had run into at Harvey's Pub out on Grand Avenue – the last of four taverns they hit that night and early morning.

"I wasn't flirting, Brandon. I was just being polite." Pauline responded.

"Well, polite doesn't mean you have to hang all over him." Brandon continued, as he moved from the living room to the kitchen to grab another beer out of the refrigerator.

"I don't think that giving my old friend – friend – a hug constitutes hanging all over him." said Pauline.

"You were acting like a fuckin whore, Pauline, and I'm sick of it!" said Brandon as he raised his voice.

"Don't you call me a whore, Brandon!" Pauline fired back.

"I call it like I see it. It looked like you wanted to fuck him!" yelled Brandon. "How do you think that makes me feel, Pauline? Its fucking humiliating! He was staring at your tits."

"What are you fucking talking about?" said Pauline.

"You know what I'm talking about! You're just a God damned whore! I don't know why I'm with you!" Brandon yelled before downing his beer.

Pauline stood from the couch and threw an empty glass at Brandon as hard as she could. The glass sailed past Brandon's head as he ducked. It smashed against the refrigerator, and tiny shards of broken glass showered all over the kitchen floor. The neighbors were now awake and hearing the whole episode. His eyes now wide open, Brandon whipped his empty beer bottle in Pauline's direction and lunged toward Pauline grabbing her by the hair. He pulled her head back violently, and the couple fell onto the living room floor.

"You bitch!" exclaimed Brandon, as he put his left hand on Pauline's throat and began to squeeze. He was holding her down.

Pauline reached up and scratched at Brandon's face raking her fingernails across his eye. Brandon reared back to protect himself and punched Pauline in the face. Pauline rolled over and curled into a fetal position. Brandon stood up and kicked her in the ribs with a hollow thud. Pauline tried to scream, but the wind had been knocked out of her. She instinctively covered her head with her hands and stayed on the floor. She was sobbing uncontrollably. Her face felt numb, and blood was flowing from her nose. She could barely breath. Brandon left the living room and walked to the bedroom.

"That'll teach you not to throw shit at me, bitch!" yelled Brandon from the bedroom.

The neighbors called 911. Five minutes later Galesburg Police were knocking on the door to apartment 121. They had been there before. Pauline, who was still laying on the floor, got up and answered the door.

"Ma'am, I'm Officer Gabe Ramirez with the Galesburg Police Department. We got a call about a domestic disturbance at this address. Are you okay?" said Officer Ramirez.

"Do I look okay?" Pauline retorted.

"Can we come in, ma'am?" asked Officer Simpson.

"Sure, don't mind me. Come on in. Please." Pauline responded.

Brandon came out of the bedroom. Seeing the police, he immediately blamed Pauline for the fracas.

"She is crazy, officer. She's not even on the lease here. She threw a glass at me. See?" said Brandon as he pointed to the broken glass on the kitchen floor.

"Calm down, sir." Officer Ramirez instructed Brandon.

The police officers each took one of the combatants to separate areas to question them and calm them down. Officer Ramirez took Pauline, still bleeding from her nose and with her left eye starting to swell. They went outside. Officer Simpson stayed inside with Brandon.

"What is your name, ma'am?" asked Officer Ramirez.

"Pauline. Pauline LoBianco." she responded.

"What happened here tonight." asked the officer.

"He beat the shit out of me. That's what happened." she explained. "I'm sick of it. This is certainly not the first time, either. I'm done. I am moving out."

Officer Ramirez continued to calm her down and ask questions. He also took photographs of Pauline's face, neck and side. Pauline had quite a story to tell, and Officer Ramirez took copious notes.

Meanwhile, Officer Simpson was inside having the same discussion with Brandon. Officer Ramirez then left Pauline outside and reentered the apartment where he spoke to Officer Simpson. The two determined that Brandon should be arrested for domestic assault. Brandon was handcuffed and escorted outside to the police car. On his way out, Brandon had a few choice words for his girlfriend. Brandon was taken to the Knox County Jail and booked. He would not be released on a notice to appear. He would need to see a judge Monday morning for bond. Officers Ramirez and Simpson then returned to the police department to complete a report.

For months, there were no legitimate responses to the Facebook post. The Department received a few responses from crackpots with clearly erroneous or absent information – real "tin foil hat" type of stuff. So, another identical post was made.

Six months later, things changed when one of the patrolmen gave Detective Franklin a police report to review.

"You might want to take a look at this, Detective." Officer Ramirez said.

"What's going on here?" asked Kolby.

"I responded to a domestic dispute last night at 1500 N. Henderson Street. You know the Henderson Manor Apartments?" said Officer Ramirez.

"And?" responded Kolby.

"And the complaining witness, a young woman who was clearly being beaten by her boyfriend, told me that she had information about the Morrissey murder at Schrodinger's Market." said Officer Ramirez. "She was very angry at her boyfriend, pressed charges and moved out of the apartment while we had him in custody."

Kolby scoured the report.

"Pauline LoBianco?" asked Kolby

"Yes. She said she had information and needed the reward to pay for attorney's fees." Responded Officer Ramirez.

Pauline had moved home to her parent's home while she looked for her own apartment. When Detective Franklin knocked on the parents' door, they answered and informed him that Pauline was at work. Kolby called Pauline at the cell number she had given to Officer Ramirez and made arrangements to meet with her after her shift at the Galesburg Police Station. Jay was traveling out of town at the time, but Kolby called Jay to let him know about the promising development.

Kolby checked Pauline's criminal record and found it was clean.

At 9:30 p.m. that night, Pauline made her way to the Department and told them she was there to see Detective Franklin. Kolby came out and escorted Pauline back into an open interview room. The room was small and cramped. The walls were made of bare, white concrete blocks. There was a camera in one corner near the ceiling. Pauline felt claustrophobic.

"Can I get you something to drink while we talk, Pauline?" asked Kolby.

"Oh no, I'm fine. Just really nervous." said Pauline.

"No reason to be nervous, Pauline, but I totally understand." said Kolby.

"Will this conversation be confidential? asked Pauline.

"I can't promise that, Pauline." said Kolby

"I'm afraid that he will kill me if he finds out what I have told you, whether it's true or not." said Pauline.

"We will absolutely protect you, Pauline. To be eligible for the reward, you will have to assist us with information necessary to arrest him and to successfully prosecute him. Do you mind if I record this interview?" said Kolby.

"I'm okay with that. I understand. I am just really afraid. He is a very violent man." said Pauline.

"Who is 'he', Pauline? Who are we talking

about?" asked Kolby as he activated the recording equipment.

"My boyfriend, Brandon. Brandon Anderson. We're separated now. I lived with him for a bit, but I have moved out. But he knows where I am staying. With my parents, but I guess you know that." said Pauline.

Kolby started taking notes.

"Brandon Anderson. That name sounds familiar. Does Brandon have a criminal record to your knowledge? I'll check after we're done, but just give me an idea." asked Kolby.

"An extensive one. He likes to beat up his girlfriends, use meth and drive drunk." said Pauline.

"What information do you have about Brandon, Pauline?" asked Kolby.

"I'm embarrassed to admit it, because I should have come forward a long time ago. But I just didn't know what to do." said Pauline as she began to cry. "I'm just so afraid."

Kolby pushed a box of tissue over the small table to her.

"Did Brandon tell you something, or did you see something?" asked Kolby.

"He told me. He told me that he was the one who robbed the Schrodinger's Market and shot the clerk, Scott Morrissey, years ago. He confessed this to me in confidence one crazy night after I agreed never to tell anyone. We had been drinking, and he just said it. Matter of fact." said Pauline.

"Okay. Did Brandon give you any details beyond that?" asked Kolby.

"No. Not that I remember. I don't know." said Pauline.

"Okay. We can work with that. I want you to keep this under your hat, right? Don't talk to anyone about this." said Kolby. "Do you know if he has any guns in the apartment?"

"He does. He has a handgun, but I can't tell you what kind it is or much about it. I don't like guns." said Pauline.

"Do you know where in the apartment he keeps it?" asked Kolby.

"The last time I saw it, it was in the bedroom. I didn't see exactly where he put it. But it was hidden somewhere. He's not supposed to have a gun because he's a felon." said Pauline.

Brandon had been arrested on domestic assault charges arising out of the incident with Pauline, and he was currently in the Knox County Jail awaiting his bond hearing. Kolby wanted to move on this information right away. He excused Pauline and escorted her out of the Department. He would ask for an extra patrol near Pauline's parent's home if and when Brandon got out of jail. But right now, he needed to get a search warrant for Brandon's apartment. Pauline no longer lived there and couldn't grant permission for the police to search it. A judge would need to issue a search warrant allowing them to enter the apartment and look for the handgun.

Kolby called Ashley Jackson, the Assistant State's Attorney on duty for search warrants that night. It was getting late, but Ashley and Kolby could take an application for a warrant to Judge Henderson at home. And they did. The Judge found probable cause existing based on the affidavit made out by Detective Franklin, and the search warrant was issued.

Kolby crossed his fingers and hoped that the gun Pauline had mentioned was there and was an FN Five-Seven. Kolby put a team together from the officers on duty that shift, and they went to the apartment and knocked, announcing they were there to execute a search warrant. No knock warrants were not popular with the courts following the Breonna Taylor case in Kentucky. As expected, there was no answer, and they breached it and made entry.

The officers made sure the apartment was clear and then spread out and began searching every room. Kolby headed for the bedroom.

"Found some dope!" yelled Officer Ramirez from the kitchen. "Looks like meth."

"I don't care about dope. We're looking for a gun." said Kolby.

After approximately fifteen minutes of searching seemingly every corner of the small one bedroom, one bath apartment, no gun had been found. Every drawer, every cushion, the mattress, the refrigerator, the closets, the clothing, the medicine cabinet, everything had been searched. Kolby sat on the bed perplexed and frustrated.

"What the fuck! Is she completely full of shit?" said Kolby wondering if he had been taken on a wild goose chase by Pauline. "Or is this asshole, Brandon, just lucky enough or smart enough to have hidden his gun somewhere else?"

"It sure wouldn't be the first time we drilled a dry hole, Detective," said Officer Ramirez.

"It's here, God damn it! It has to be here." said Kolby as he rechecked places he had already searched. Then he took another look at the small bedroom closet. He looked at the ceiling, and then he pounded on the floor and was met by a very hollow rattle. There was an area of the floor that was loose. He grabbed his pocketknife and started prying at the floor in that area, and a crack appeared. He pulled up on that loose piece and shone his flashlight into the shallow hole.

"There's that son of a bitch." said Kolby, as he pulled out an object wrapped in a silicon gun cloth.

He unwrapped the cloth, and his face lit up.

"Here it is! An FN Five-Seven. I'll be damned. Ten bucks says this is the gun used to kill Scott Morrissey." said Kolby.

Kolby had never actually handled an FN Five-Seven. He pulled the magazine out of it, racked the slide and looked into the chamber to clear it. But he had seen pictures of them, and it was clearly marked. Kolby had a very good feeling that this find, together with Pauline's testimony, was going to secure a conviction and solve this case. After a brief celebration by the search team, the search warrant was returned, and the firearm was placed in an evidence locker at the Police Department. Kolby called ASA Ashley Jackson to share the good news and to begin the process of filing charges against Brandon Anderson for the murder of Scott Morrissey. They clearly had enough to charge him with unlawful possession of a firearm by a felon and for the drug possession, but Ashley wanted to see if any additional evidence could be obtained to further corroborate his alleged confession.

Monday, Kolby arranged to interview Brandon in the jail only to discover that Brandon had been released from jail by posting bond, which had been set at a ridiculously low amount of $5,000. Brandon had only been required to put up ten percent or $500 of cash bail to secure his release. He had been able to talk one of his friends into paying the bail. Kolby was immediately back on the phone with Ashley seeking an arrest warrant for Brandon on the gun and drug charges, at least. Finding him was going to be interesting, as he now knew the police were on to him. The condition of his apartment, the missing gun and the search warrant would make that clear. He was going to go after Pauline.

With an arrest warrant issued, Kolby called Pauline to let her know Brandon was out and probably suspected that she had ratted on him about the gun, dope and possibly the murder. She told Kolby that she was already aware. Brandon's bond order prohibited him from contacting Pauline, but neither Kolby nor Pauline trusted that piece of paper would be effective, especially given Brandon's history of violating an order of protection. Kolby reiterated that he would have an extra patrol put on her parent's house and the restaurant and that they were looking to arrest him again on new charges.

"We will find him, Pauline, and we will arrest him, and I believe with your help he is going away for a long time." Kolby assured her.

Kolby sent officers to KFC and the apartment to see if they could find Brandon. He also contacted the Knox County Sheriff's Department to ask that a deputy go to Altona to Brandon's parents' home there to see if he had gone there.

Officer Todd Scott turned his patrol car west onto Tompkins Street off of Academy Street. He was patrolling the south side of town. He saw a vehicle that fit the description of Brandon Anderson's, and he saw two men standing on the terrace near the car. Given the neighborhood, this was most likely a drug deal. Officer Scott brought his car to a stop and shone his light on the two men. Before he could roll down his window, the taller man took off running on foot. Officer Scott quickly exited his car and gave chase. Officer Scott was young and in tremendous shape and was able to overtake the suspect in the backyard of a boarded-up house three lots down the block. He tackled the suspect and took him to the ground, hard.

"What is your name?" asked Officer Scott as he handcuffed the man.

"Brandon Anderson. What did I do?" said the man clearly out of breath.

Kolby's phone rang.

"We found that piece of shit, Franklin." exclaimed the officer on the other end.

"You've got Brandon Anderson?" asked Kolby.

"I found him on Thompkins Street attempting to score a bag of meth. The douchebag tried to run, but I was able to run him down." said Officer Scott.

"Well, of course Tompkins Street was his first stop. He has his priorities straight." Kolby said sarcastically. "Excellent work!"

Back to the Knox County Jail went Brandon Anderson. This time his bond would be significantly higher, and Kolby wasn't going to wait to interview him. He made arrangements to do so immediately.

As Kolby walked down to the interview room where Brandon had been secured, he ran into Attorney Marsha Davis of McClay & Davis LLC. His heart sank.

"Detective Franklin, I'm Marsha Davis, and I represent Brandon Anderson." said Marsha.

"As you might imagine, I have some questions for Brandon." said Kolby.

"Well, I will be sitting in on the interview, and I may terminate the interview. We'll just have to see." said Marsha.

The two entered the interview room, and with the consent of all, Kolby activated the recording equipment. Marsha introduced herself to her client, as they had not yet met. Brandon's parents had hired Marsha to represent their son on the gun and meth charges. Nobody had apparently told Marsha about the possibility of murder charges, and she hadn't yet met with Brandon. Brandon was likely thinking that Kolby knew nothing about the robbery and murder. This was going to be interesting.

Kolby informed Brandon of his Miranda rights and had Brandon sign the waiver before the questioning began. He asked him if he wanted an opportunity to confer with his attorney, and Brandon declined. Marsha did not insist. Apparently, they were planning on winging it.

"You're Brandon Anderson, correct? And you live at the Henderson Manor Apartments, No. 121, on North Henderson Street in Galesburg, is that right?"

asked Kolby

"Correct." said Brandon.

"Until just recently, you resided there with your then girlfriend, Pauline LoBianco?" asked Kolby.

"That's right. She made up some bullshit about me hitting her and moved out." said Brandon.

"Pauline told us a few things about you, and we searched your apartment. Are you aware of that?" asked Kolby.

"I figured." said Brandon.

Marsha had surely read the arrest warrant and spoken with the State's Attorney's Office to discover that the charges involved a gun and some meth.

"We found a handgun in your apartment, are you aware of that?" asked Kolby.

"That's what I understand." said Brandon.

"We ran the serial number on the that gun, and it came back stolen. It turns out that someone in Galesburg reported that gun stolen over ten years ago." stated Kolby.

"Okay." said Brandon.

"We ran a fingerprint test on the gun, and your fingerprints were on it, the magazine and the shell casings." stated Kolby, making that fact up.

"Okay." said Brandon.

"Are you surprised by either of those facts?"

asked Kolby.

"I'm not surprised by the fingerprints. That's my gun. I am surprised that it is stolen. I purchased that gun off of a guy a few years ago. I had no idea it was stolen." said Brandon.

"Do you remember the name of the person you purchased it from?" asked Kolby.

"No. It's been so long. It was just some guy here in Galesburg." said Brandon.

"Did you use a firearms transfer form?" asked Kolby.

"A what?" asked Brandon.

"Do you recall where the man lived?" asked Kolby.

"No." said Brandon.

"Do you remember where you were when you purchased the gun?" asked Kolby.

"Not off the top of my head." said Brandon.

"You do understand that as a felon you are prohibited by law from possessing a firearm, right?" asked Kolby, surprised that Marsha was letting him go there.

"I'm not a lawyer. I don't know exactly what the law says on that." Brandon answered.

"And you know that we found a good quantity of methamphetamines in your apartment?" asked

Kolby.

"Right. That was all Pauline's stuff that she left when she moved out." said Brandon.

"Do you think Pauline would corroborate you on that?" asked Kolby.

"Of course not, she's a lying bitch. She's out to get me. She's got a vendetta against me or something. She's nuts." said Brandon.

"You know what else Pauline told us?" asked Kolby.

"I can only imagine what kind of crap she came up with." said Brandon.

"Pauline told us that you confessed to her that you murdered Scott Morrissey at Schrodinger's Market in 2008." stated Kolby.

"Okay, we're done here." Marsha interjected. "This interview is terminated."

"That's bullshit!" exclaimed Brandon.

"Nope that's it. We're not answering any more questions." said Marsha.

"She's a lying sack of dogshit! I can't believe she said something like that. One of you is lying." said Brandon.

"Brandon don't say anything else. We're done." said Marsha as she stood up.

"Before you go, you should know that the ballistics of your gun match that of the bullet that killed Scott Morrissey." said Kolby.

"I will discuss this case with the State's Attorney's Office, Detective Franklin. My client is hereby invoking his right to remain silent. There will be no more interrogation of him." said Marsha.

Marsha left the room. Kolby turned off the recording equipment and slumped in his chair. Brandon was taken back to the jail. With Brandon's admission that it was his gun, Ashley would likely file a criminal complaint against Brandon for robbery and murder.

The next day, Ashley called Pauline into the State's Attorney's Office at the Knox County Courthouse to get a sense for herself about how credible Pauline would be and if there was any additional information she could provide. She explained to Pauline that she would be the State's key witness in the prosecution of Brandon Anderson for robbery and murder. Pauline understood, and she promised to stick to her guns. Ashley was convinced. She felt that she had enough to prove the robbery and murder charges beyond a reasonable doubt. It was not perfect, but she knew that perfect was the enemy of good. Shortly thereafter, Ashley took the case to the grand jury which, in turn, returned an indictment against Brandon for the robbery of Schrodinger's Market and the murder of Scott Morrissey.

Kolby and Jay made arrangements to meet with Lin Kim to give her the great news. It looked like the

State had the right man, and he had been charged with the crime. Lin was ecstatic over the news.

Bond was reset at an unattainable level, and Brandon, accompanied by his attorney Marsha Davis, entered a plea of not guilty and demanded a jury trial.

Marsha called Ashley.

"Ashley, its Marsha Davis. I'm calling you about the Brandon Anderson case." said Marsha.

"Hello Marsha. How are you doing? Sorry I missed you this morning when you stopped by the office." said Ashley.

"No sweat. I just wanted to touch base with you about this case. I like to meet in person when I can to have these types of discussions" said Marsha.

"I have some time available this afternoon. I'm happy to come down to your office and we can talk." said Ashley.

"Sounds good. Can you be here at 2:00?" asked Marsha.

"Sure. See you then." said Ashley.

Marsha had spoken with Brandon about the process of settlement. She had been given the entire file on the case compiled by the State's Attorney's Office, as was their obligation under the law. Now it was time to find out what the State was willing to offer for a plea bargain. Given Brandon's criminal record and the nature of the crimes in this case, there was a lot of room for negotiation on how to resolve this case. Both sides knew it.

At 2:00 p.m. sharp, Ashley walked through the front door of the offices of McClay & Davis, LLC. Ashley was young, but she was a seasoned prosecutor. She had joined the Knox County State's Attorney's Office from a private practice of criminal defense. She had been an ASA for ten years and shared responsibility with another Assistant for prosecuting major felony cases. She was confident, and her posture and gait were consistent with that.

"Ashley." Marsha greeted her.

"Your offices are so beautiful, Marsha." said Ashley as she looked around the large waiting area.

"Thank you, Ashley! Matthew and I finally remodeled last year. It turned out well." said Marsha.

"It sure did!" said Ashley. "As you know our offices in the Courthouse leave something to be desired."

"Let's go into my office." said Marsha as the two walked down the hallway past Matthew's office and the conference room."

"Where's your library now, Marsha?" asked Ashley.

"Oh, we're completely online now. We don't subscribe to the reporters or bound statutes anymore. So, we freed up the old library to serve as a real estate closing room. It's great." explained Marsha.

The two entered Marsha's spacious and well-appointed office, decorated very tastefully, and Ashley sat in front of the desk in one of the two comfortable client chairs.

"Tell me what you're thinking on this file." asked Marsha as she sat behind her desk.

"I'm thinking we have from twenty years to life imprisonment to work with here. Given the defendant's extensive criminal record, the State would like to see a sentence of forty years on the murder charge, and the robbery, gun and drug charges would be dismissed." stated Ashley.

"Well, you have to give me something to work with here, Ashley. My client would be about seventy-two years old when he got out if he served the full sentence. That's is a lot longer than most murder sentences." Marsha responded.

"I think we have a pretty solid case on all counts, including first degree murder, Marsha. So, I'm not interested in discounting the sentence too much based upon a chance of an acquittal." said Ashley.

Marsha moved into the client chair beside Ashley.

"Ashley, my guy has never been in prison before. He is not going to agree to go to prison for forty years when the worst-case scenario for him is life, which is probably not much longer. I mean, his life expectancy as a Caucasian male is only about seventy-eight years according to the mortality tables. He's thirty-two. You're suggesting that he agree to essentially a life sentence." said Marsha.

"What's your proposal, Marsha? I don't want to bid against myself." said Ashley.

"I was thinking twenty years on a lesser charge so that he can qualify for a "good time" reduction. I think I can sell that. Dismiss all but a lesser included charge of manslaughter." suggested Marsha.

"Yeah. That's not going to happen. I will consider thirty years on a first-degree murder charge." said Ashley.

"I will have to talk to my client. I don't think you're sufficiently discounting your case for the possibility that you may lose. All you have is the word of a disgruntled ex-girlfriend and a gun similar to the one used. I can drive a truck through the reasonable doubt hole in that case, Ashley." said Marsha.

"Pauline LoBianco has a spotless record, Marsha. It will be very difficult to impeach her credibility. She's disgruntled for good reason." replied Ashley.

"Why did it take her years to come forward - and then only when she saw the chance for a $10,000 reward? I don't see that as a slam dunk case for the State." said Marsha.

"If you come to me with an offer for twenty-five years on a second-degree murder charge, I'll seriously consider it, Marsha." stated Ashley.

"I'll get back to you, okay? I have some work to do to get there if I can." said Marsha, as she stood to escort Ashley from her office.

Ashley had spoken with Scott Morrissey's surviving mother in Clayton, Missouri about the case. Marjorie Morrissey didn't understand why Illinois no longer had a death penalty like Missouri. She was not happy with any sentence less than life for the scumbag who killed her baby boy. But Ashley had explained the plea-bargaining process to her, a speech Ashley has made hundreds of times before. And Mrs. Morrissey seemed to understand and would be supportive of any outcome that put Brandon Anderson behind bars for a substantial period time. She agreed that was better than the chance that Brandon might go free on an acquittal.

On the other hand, Marsha Davis had an uphill battle ahead of her. It is a delicate balance for a criminal defense lawyer. You need to make sure to avoid appearing to take the other side. Trying to convince your client of the strength of the State's case can have that effect. "Whose side are you on?" you often hear. By the same token, you have to impart to your client the knowledge you have accumulated through your education and experience about how the system works and what the probable outcome is going to be. You don't want your client to make such a crucial decision without the best information. It's a tough gambit. At the end of the day, it is the client's decision to make, and you have to represent them the best you can, given the decisions they have made. Marsha was a master at it.

Marsha dropped into the Knox County Jail and arranged to meet with her client in one of the confidential meeting rooms. Brandon had admitted to Marsha in confidence under attorney-client privilege that he had been the one who robbed Schrodinger's Market and shot Scott Morrissey to death on June 15, 2008. That didn't really change the way she planned to handle his defense. She was certainly not going to put him on the witness stand to testify. His extensive criminal record would give the State an absolute field day on cross-examination. Neither was she going to put forth any type of affirmative defense or argument that some other particular individual had done it. Rather, the plan was simply to hold the State to its high burden of proving its case beyond a reasonable doubt.

"How are ya, Marsha?" asked Brandon.

"I'd ask the same of you, Brandon, but I think I know the answer." said Marsha.

"Yeah. This place sucks bad." said Brandon.

"Well, that's why I'm here today, Brandon. I think I have an opportunity to settle this case in a way which will significantly reduce the amount of time you need to spend incarcerated." said Marsha.

"Really? Is the State willing to dismiss the case?" asked Brandon.

"Well, not exactly, but I think I can get them

to dismiss all but a second-degree murder charge and agree to a sentence of twenty-five years. That would allow you to serve considerably less than twenty-five years with good time credit." said Marsha.

"Well, that sounds like shit to me. I can't survive in here, Marsha. I can't survive for a month let alone a year or ten years or twenty-five years. I can't do it." said Brandon.

"Brandon, I understand, but if they win – and they probably will – they are going to ask the court to sentence you to life in prison. Even if the court gave you forty years, you would have to serve the whole forty-year sentence. No credit for good time. You would be an old man by the time you got out." explained Marsha.

"Well, we will just have to win then. Isn't that what my parents are paying you $250 per hour for?" asked Brandon.

"No, Brandon. That is not what I am here for. I am here to help you obtain the best outcome possible under the circumstances. If we can't win this case – and that is a real probability – then I need to try to get you the best deal I can. Of course, it is up to you to make the decisions on these things, but I hope you will take my advice. I have been doing this a long time." said Marsha emphatically.

"There has to be another way." pleaded Brandon.

"Of course, anything is possible, and there is a very slim chance that you might win if we tried this case to a jury. Very slim. In that event, you would walk free. But you would have to beat all of the charges: the gun charges, the drug charges, the robbery charge and the murder charge. That's just not going to happen, Brandon." Marsha predicted.

"What if I had something to offer the State's Attorney?" asked Brandon.

"Do you have any information to offer?" asked Marsha.

"Not really." Brandon admitted.

"I really think you need to consider my advice, Brandon. I will give you some time to think it over and come to a decision. But I think you need to authorize me to make an offer to the State to plead guilty or no contest to a second-degree murder charge in exchange for a sentence of twenty-five years. It's not going to get any better than that." said Marsha as she called to let the jailors know that their meeting was over.

"I really appreciate what you're doing for me. Don't get me wrong, Marsha. I just can't imagine being in prison that long. I just have to think about it." said Brandon.

"Let me know when you want to talk again, okay?" said Marsha, thinking to herself "If you can't do the time, then don't do the crime, Sonny."

"I will, Marsha. Thanks." said Brandon.

Lin occasionally touched base with Kolby to get a status report on the Brandon Anderson case. She was anxious to pay Pauline her $10,000 reward. She was very pleased that things seemed to be going so well. She did not obsess, however. Lin kept very busy. She was helping to manage the market, she was still working thirty hours a week at the Art Center, she was teaching Art to the Knox Students, and she found time to paint and catch up with the girls by phone and text.

At Schrodinger's Market, Josh was doing an excellent job operating the store, and he seemed to be enjoying himself. Sarah was starting to come to Galesburg once in awhile to save Josh the long drive to Carbondale. Josh and Lin had agreed to some over-due upgrades to the store. Revenues had been steady, although expenses had increased slightly now that an additional employee had been added to the payroll. Glen had not taken a large salary, and Lin took no salary. Wage rates and inflation had begun to rise, which further cut into the store's profits. But the store was profitable, nevertheless, even with the salary increase Lin had suggested for Josh. The two split the profits periodically.

The Art Center was doing well. Lin had organized a wonderful staff of volunteers, and the Center was basically on autopilot. All of the shows, fundraisers and other events were planned for the coming year. She was particularly excited about a couple of programs scheduled and thought they would be a big hit with the community.

Lin was getting tired of teaching at Knox, however. The students were becoming so extreme in their politics and behavior that she no longer felt appreciated by them and didn't feel that she was imparting to them knowledge and skills they truly cared about. She didn't fit in. Over the years, the college had spiraled into a bizarre collection of extremely liberal students and faculty. The more liberal the current students got, the more liberal the new students got, and the process continued to cycle to the point of absurdity. No student who visited the campus would even consider going to Knox unless they were a full-blown Marxist or Anarchist. Faculty recruiting and tenure decisions reflected the same philosophy. Only the most radical left were hired or promoted. Of course, the Art students tended to be the very most left leaning of the student body. Even though Lin steadfastly maintained her politics as private, she did not actively support any of the student or faculty initiatives or activities. Nor did she engage her students in conversations about culture, philosophy or social issues. She just didn't see the world the same way they did. It was wearing on her.

Lin's painting had become prolific. She was working toward a show at a Museum in Peoria. She was also painting a large portrait of Scott Morrissey from a photograph Glen had taken of him at the store. That piece would not be for sale at the show.

Kolby Franklin was riding high in light of his good fortune in the Brandon Anderson case. He was confident that the State would obtain either a guilty plea or a verdict convicting Brandon of the crimes that had so deeply disturbed Glen. That was poised to come to closure at some point in the near future, he thought. He was getting high marks as a detective at the Galesburg Police Department. Moreover, Kolby now had a girlfriend. Perfectly suited for Kolby, she was an actuary at State Farm in Bloomington, Illinois but worked remotely from Galesburg. For the first time, Kolby had found someone who appreciated his math stories and musings. He attributed the attraction to electromagnetism.

Jay Ashworth was busy in his private investigations business. The firm gave him a steady diet of work, from service of process to obtaining witness statements and performing background investigations. He also had the occasional case brought to him by private parties -- a concerned husband wanting to know whether his wife was cheating or a parent wanting to make sure her daughter wasn't dating the wrong kid. Lin had settled up with him weeks ago, and both had been very happy with the fees. Lin had thought them very reasonable, and Jay had enjoyed a particularly good month as a result.

Ashley was busy interviewing the County Medical Examiner and ballistics expert from the Illinois State Police in preparation for the Brandon Anderson trial. She planned to spend some time preparing the Galesburg Police Department officers and detectives who had investigated the crime ten years ago and those that had solved it most recently. Finally, Ashley was in regular contact with Pauline to make sure she wasn't going weak kneed on her. Her testimony was critical to the case, and Ashley had a considerable amount of experience with complaining witnesses folding, recanting and going back to their abusive mates. If Pauline had such a change of heart, the case against Brandon would evaporate.

Pauline was struggling with being alone. She was unable to find an apartment or rental home she could afford on her own, and she didn't have any friends who were candidates for a roommate. She was still living with her parents. At thirty, she was mortified about that. However, the hardest thing was how much she longed for Brandon. She loved him. That love does not dissipate overnight. She was angry with him for the way that he treated her, particularly when he was intoxicated, which was quite often. But she adored the way he made her feel when they made up and during the good times. She had written, and then crumpled and discarded, many letters to Brandon in jail. She was heartbroken that he was in jail because of things she had said. She didn't want him to hate her. She considered her options and what would happen if she told Detective Franklin and Ashley Jackson that she had made a big mistake. Would she be forced to testify anyway? Would the State move forward? What if Brandon was really capable of killing someone? But Pauline had nobody to share her feelings with. Her parents and friends were adamant that she have nothing to do with him and that she testify against him, if necessary. She knew the right thing to do. It was just really hard.

Two weeks later, Marsha got a message from her administrative assistant that Brandon had called for her. He had left a brief message that he wanted to talk. Marsha talked to Matthew McClay about the status of her negotiations with the State in the case. Matthew agreed with Marsha's assessment, and that buoyed her even more. She made arrangements to meet with Brandon again at the jail.

"Thank you for coming." Brandon started.

"You're more than welcome, Brandon." said Marsha. "What are your thoughts at this point."

"I want to take the deal. I want to follow your advice and take the plea deal you suggested." said Brandon, surprising Marsha.

"Is that what you truly want, Brandon? Nobody's pressuring you, are they?" asked Marsha.

"That is what I want to do. I don't feel I have any real option. I could insist on a trial, but I trust your judgment on that. I don't feel we can win that no matter how hard we fight. I don't want to do this for the rest of my life. I want to take the deal." said Brandon.

"Very well. Let me see if I can get this put to bed along those lines, Brandon. I will let you know as soon as possible." said Marsha.

Marsha didn't have the heart to warn him that

Ashley had simply solicited an offer of this type from the defendant and said she would consider it. It wasn't a done deal yet. And the judge would have to accept the plea, but Marsha was less concerned about that. Marsha went back to the office and called Ashley. Ashley answered.

"Hey Ashley. It's Marsha." said Marsha.

"Hi Marsha. Are you calling on the Anderson case or the Simpson case?" asked Ashley.

"I wanted to follow up with you on Brandon Anderson." said Marsha.

"Are we going to be able to get something done on that case, Marsha?" asked Ashley.

"It looks like it. My client has authorized me to enter into a plea deal where he pleads guilty or no contest to second degree murder, all other charges being dismissed, in exchange for a twenty- five-year sentence." said Marsha.

Ashley was surprised and very pleased, but she didn't let on.

"I will do that, Marsha. I can accept that deal. Let's get him in front of the court before he changes his mind." said Ashley.

"I hear ya, Ashley. Let's get it done." said Marsha.

Two days later, Brandon was brought over from the Courthouse by the Sheriff's Department, and he was taken into the courtroom. Ashley, Marsha, the bailiff and the court reporter were in the courtroom. Brandon saw his mother and father sitting far apart from a couple of other people Brandon assumed were reporters. He was wrong. The two women in the front row were Lin Kim and Marjorie Morrissey, the two people in this world who wanted to see him go to prison for the longest period possible. They stared at him intently until he could feel their gaze. He turned to look at them as he sat. He was in an orange shirt and pants with flipflops. He was fully shackled, wrists and ankles. Detective Kolby Franklin was also present. He was standing with the Sheriff's Deputies, catching up.

When Judge Walker entered, the bailiff asked that all rise. The judge then asked everyone to be seated.

"Let the record show that these proceedings are in State v. Brandon Anderson, 2021-CF-47. Do I understand that the parties have reached a plea agreement in this matter?" said the Judge, as the court reporter took it down.

"We have, Your Honor." said Ashley.

"That is correct, Judge Walker." said Marsha.

"Alright. Mrs. Jackson will you please inform the Court what the terms of that plea agreement are?" asked the Judge.

"Your Honor, Defendant, Mr. Anderson, has

agreed to enter an Alford plea admitting that the State's evidence is sufficient to prove beyond a reasonable doubt that he committed the offense of second-degree murder in Knox County, Illinois on June 15, 2008 by the homicide of Scott Morrissey. In exchange, the State has agreed to dismiss all other counts of the Complaint and recommend a sentence of twenty-five years in the Department of Corrections." said Ashley.

"Ms. Davis does that accurately state the terms of the plea agreement?" asked the Judge.

"It does, Your Honor." said Marsha.

"Very well, Mr. Anderson will you please step forward? Have counsel accurately stated the agreement you have reached?" asked the Judge.

"Yes, Judge." stated Brandon.

"I understand then that you wish to change your plea of not guilty, is that right?" asked the Judge.

"Yes, Judge." stated Brandon.

"Has anyone promised you anything, other than as set forth in the plea agreement itself, to get you to change your plea?" asked the Judge.

"No, Your Honor." stated Brandon.

"Has anyone threatened or coerced you to change your plea?" asked the Judge.

"No, Your Honor." stated Brandon.

"Mrs. Jackson, will you please state the State's

case on which Defendant will enter an Alford plea?" asked the Judge.

"Of course, Your Honor. State's witness, Pauline LoBianco, will testify that on or about September 14, 2014, Defendant confessed to her, his then girlfriend, that he had robbed the Schrodinger's Market in downtown Galesburg and had shot the clerk, Scott Morrissey, to death. Officer Wilbur Johnson will testify that on June 15, 2008, he was dispatched to said location where he found Scott Morrissey dead having been shot one time in the head. The County Medical Examiner will testify that Scott Morrissey died as the result of that single gunshot wound. The Illinois State Police Ballistics Scientist will testify that the caliber of the single bullet discovered at the scene embedded in the wall where Mr. Morrissey had been shot was the very unusual 5.7x28, which is only fired by one firearm, the FN Five-Seven handgun. Detective Kolby Franklin will testify that he recovered a FN Five-Seven handgun from Defendant's apartment pursuant to a search warrant and that Defendant had admitted to him that he owned the handgun." stated Ashley.

"Does Defendant agree that the State's evidence would likely result in a guilty verdict if the case were tried?" asked the Judge.

"Yes, Your Honor." stated Marsha.

"Is that your plea at this time, Mr. Anderson?" asked the Judge

"Yes, it is, Judge." said Brandon.

The Judge then informed Brandon of his rights regarding his plea.

"Do you understand what I have just explained to you?" asked the Judge.

"Yes, Judge." answered Brandon.

"You have had the benefit of counsel in this matter and during the course of this plea agreement?" asked the Judge.

"Yes, Judge." said Brandon.

"Do you have any questions for the Court, Mr. Anderson?" asked the Judge.

"No, Judge." stated Brandon.

"Okay. I accept the plea agreement. I hereby find you guilty of second-degree murder in the death of Scott Morrissey, and I hereby impose a sentence of incarceration in the Illinois Department of Corrections for a period of twenty-five years. The defendant is remanded to the custody of the Department." stated the Judge.

The Sheriff's Jailors took Brandon back into custody and ushered him out of the courtroom into the hall and down the elevator. Brandon's parents were both sobbing. So was Mrs. Morrissey. It had taken ten years, but they had finally found him, she thought. The experience had dredged up the horror she had suffered so many years ago the night she was contacted by the police and told about her only son's awful fate. Lin was not tearful. She seemed satisfied, like she had helped to bring balance back to the universe, that she had just done something very meaningful and impactful. She was proud. She thought of how Glen would have reacted. Maybe it would have restored Glen's trust in law enforcement. She thought of Kolby and Jay and how important they had been in this process. And she thought of Scott, who Glen had loved, trusted and treated like a son.

"Marjorie, I have something for you. It's down in my car." said Lin.

"What? What is it?" asked Marjorie.

"Come outside with me, Marjorie. I have something to give you." stated Lin.

The two women exited the courtroom, went down the elevator to the first floor and left through the security checkpoint out the front doors of the Courthouse. Lin had parked her SUV quite near the entrance in the parking area. Lin raised the back of her SUV and removed a large but thin rectangular package wrapped in tan paper.

"This is yours." Lin said as she handed the package to Marjorie.

Marjorie looked stunned.

"What is this, Lin?" Marjorie asked.

"Open it. You'll see." said Lin.

Marjorie wrestled with the wrapping paper and tape and finally tore it off to disclose its contents. It was the portrait of Scott painted by Lin in her home studio. It was beautiful. Marjorie melted. She broke down in tears again and held the painting to her chest.

"Oh my! This is absolutely wonderful, Lin. This is absolutely the way I want to remember Scott. Thank you so much, Lin." said Marjorie.

Lin saw Detective Franklin leaving the Courthouse and returning to his car parked on the street.

"I've got something else I need to take care of Marjorie." said Lin. "You're more than welcome to come back to my home with me before making the drive home."

"No thank you, Lin. I think I will get on the road now. Thank you so much for what you have done for me, Lin. I can never repay you for what you have given me and my son." said Marjorie.

"Drive safe, Marjorie. If there is ever anything I can do for you, you let me know." said Lin

Marjorie nodded and turned to walk toward her car with her painting. Lin jogged toward Kolby.

"Kolby!" Lin yelled.

Kolby spun around and started walking toward Lin.

"Kolby, where do I find Pauline LoBianco? I want to pay her the reward." asked Lin.

"How about I take you to her, Lin? Come on, I'll drive you." offered Kolby.

Lin hopped in with Kolby, who made a quick call, and the two shot over to Pauline's parent's residence. Lin knocked on the front door, and Pauline answered.

"Lin, this is Pauline. Pauline, meet Lin." said Kolby as he introduced the two for the first time.

"You are one strong woman, Pauline. It is a pleasure to finally meet you. I have something for you. Something that you have truly earned." said Lin with an outstretched arm.

Lin handed Pauline a check for $10,000. Pauline was filled with swirling and competing emotions. She thanked Pauline politely and retreated back into the home where she broke down in tears.

"That's true courage, Kolby." said Lin. Kolby agreed.

The two drove back to the Courthouse for Lin to get her car, and both went their separate ways.

The McClays divorced, as often happens following the death of a child. The trauma of the civil case following the harrowing death of their daughter proved too much for their marriage. Matthew moved out and into an apartment above his law offices downtown. With alimony from Matthew, Jamie was able to keep the big house, which made no sense because the two boys were now grown and on their own: Clyde working for the City; and Carter attending college at Drake University. All of them missed Johna terribly.

Amos Robinson retired. He and his wife, Susan, moved permanently into their summer lake house at Oak Run nearby. Amos wanted to keep the house in town, but Susan won out. Amos now spent considerably more time with his wife, adult children and grandchildren. The lake house was alive with activity, and Amos was in good health and able to enjoy the family time. He didn't miss his practice very much, although he did miss Carolyn and Kelly. Mainly he missed the sublime feeling he got from championing the case of a truly good and deserving client. He often thought of Glen Kim.

Lin had spent only $15,000 on the project. She still had $85,000 left to do with as she pleased. She was going to pay the girls back $50,000, and that left her with $35,000 to spend. Her next call was to local artist, Ralph Smith.

"Ralph, this is Lin Kim. How much would it be for you to do a life-sized sculpture of Glen hugging Johna McClay in heaven? I want to place it at Glen's grave." stated Lin.

It was late evening, and Schrodinger's Market was all lit up inside. Four tumultuous years had passed since Johna was killed. Fourteen years had passed since Scott was killed. It was Fall again, and the beautiful trees were starting to lose their leaves. What was the future for those associated with the market? It was hard to say. As he drove by it, Detective Franklin could see Josh Hernandez inside behind the counter tending to customers. Kolby was listening to "Bittersweet Symphony" by the Verve in his truck and had the volume up.

One of the most interesting things about quantum physics is that it is impossible to predict with certainty the outcome of a single experiment on a quantum system. Instead, when a physicist predicts the outcome of an experiment, the prediction takes the form of the probability for each of the possible outcomes. Kolby thought of the market as a quantum system. The two robberies at the market had each been a cruel experiment on this quantum system. Both robberies had produced very different outcomes, but the common denominator was that someone was killed, and someone went to prison. There were awful twists of fate, as well. Had Scott not been killed, Glen would probably not have had a gun in the store. If Glen had not had a gun in the store, Johna would probably not have been shot. Had Matthew not defended Kyle, Kyle probably wouldn't have been free to rob the market, causing Glen to shoot Johna.

Kolby thought about what future experiments might befall the market and the infinite possible outcomes. What forces were at work tonight which, unbeknownst to all, might impact Schrodinger's Market in the future? Kolby sang along with his radio, as he negotiated the square in downtown Galesburg and headed home.

Made in the USA
Las Vegas, NV
10 December 2021

37001452R00115